"I'm not moving anywhere."

"Of course you are. To San Jose with me. How else can I take charge of you and the baby?"

Ashley took a breath. "I don't need you taking charge. I can handle this on my own."

Jason stared at her. "I seem to recall that I was in that bed with you."

A startling heat suffused her at the memory. She looked his way and saw he was remembering, too.

She suppressed erotic images. "I'm prepared to take care of everything."

"This is my baby as much as yours," Jason countered. "You expect me to turn my back on it?"

"No, I just…"

Somehow his hand was on her arm, his fingers curling around, his thumb stroking. His focus had returned to her mouth, and if she didn't break that visual contact, she was certain he'd kiss her….

Dear Reader,

This beautiful month of April we have six very special reads for you, starting with *Falling for the Boss* by Elizabeth Harbison, this month's installment in our FAMILY BUSINESS continuity. Watch what happens when two star-crossed high school sweethearts get a second chance—only this time they're on opposite sides of the boardroom table! Next, bestselling author RaeAnne Thayne pays us a wonderful and emotional visit in Special Edition with her new miniseries, THE COWBOYS OF COLD CREEK. In *Light the Stars,* the first book in the series, a frazzled single father is shocked to hear that his mother (not to mention babysitter) eloped—with a supposed scam artist. So what is he to do when said scam artist's lovely daughter turns up on his doorstep? Find out (and don't miss next month's book in this series, *Dancing in the Moonlight*). In Patricia McLinn's *What Are Friends For?*, the first in her SEASONS IN A SMALL TOWN duet, a female police officer is reunited—with the guy who got away. Maybe she'll be able to detain him this time....

Jessica Bird concludes her MOOREHOUSE LEGACY series with *From the First,* in which Alex Moorehouse finally might get the woman he could never stop wanting. Only problem is, she's a recent widow—and her late husband was Alex's best friend. In Karen Sandler's *Her Baby's Hero,* a couple looks for that happy ending even though the second time they meet, she's six months' pregnant with his twins! And in *The Last Cowboy* by Crystal Green, a woman desperate for motherhood learns that "the last cowboy will make you a mother." But real cowboys don't exist anymore...or do they?

So enjoy, and don't forget to come back next month. Everything will be in bloom....

Have fun.

Gail Chasan
Senior Editor

Please address questions and book requests to:
Silhouette Reader Service
U.S.: 3010 Walden Ave., P.O. Box 1325, Buffalo, NY 14269
Canadian: P.O. Box 609, Fort Erie, Ont. L2A 5X3

HER BABY'S HERO

KAREN SANDLER

SPECIAL EDITION

Published by Silhouette Books

America's Publisher of Contemporary Romance

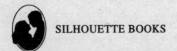 SILHOUETTE BOOKS

ISBN 0-373-24751-6

HER BABY'S HERO

Copyright © 2006 by Karen Sandler

Visit Silhouette Books at www.eHarlequin.com

Printed in U.S.A.

Books by Karen Sandler

Silhouette Special Edition

The Boss's Baby Bargain #1488
Counting on a Cowboy #1572
A Father's Sacrifice #1636
His Baby To Love #1686
The Three-Way Miracle #1733
Her Baby's Hero #1751

KAREN SANDLER

first caught the writing bug at age nine when, as a horse-crazy fourth grader, she wrote a poem about a pony named Tony. Many years of hard work later, she sold her first book (and she got that pony—although his name is Ben). She enjoys writing novels, short stories and screenplays and has produced two short films. She lives in Northern California with her husband of twenty-three years and two sons who are busy eating her out of house and home. You can reach Karen at karen@karensandler.net.

To all the kids who are different, who can't sit still in class, whose ideas would never fit inside a box.

Prologue

What had she done?

Clutching the covers to her naked body, Ashley Rand stared at Jason Kerrigan's stony profile and tried to reason through what had just happened. Five minutes ago she was moaning with passion, now she wanted to shrink inside herself as the awkwardness washed over her.

His eyes fixed on the ceiling, he wouldn't even look at her. Just as well; she wasn't sure she could meet his gaze herself. They'd come to his apartment to drown their sorrows with a pizza and a couple beers, not jump into bed. Somehow a soothing neck rub had turned into torrid sex with a man she wasn't even sure she liked half the time.

What now? Did she get up and get dressed, see if the pizza was still edible? Talk to him, make a joke about what they'd just done together?

She shut her eyes, wishing she could vanish and reappear in the ramshackle house she shared with three other women near the UC Berkeley campus. No chance she'd be able to creep into her bedroom unnoticed by her roommates, even at 2:00 a.m. They'd want all the gory details. But she didn't understand the insanity of this interlude with Jason herself, never mind being able to muster an explanation for the avid audience of her housemates.

She glanced over at Jason again. She still couldn't wrap her mind around what she was doing in bed with him.

Her friendship with the prickly, straitlaced twenty-eight-year-old grad student had arisen more through happenstance than common interest. They both tutored at-risk kids at a local high school. When Ashley's finicky VW had broken down, Jason had offered her a ride. He'd all but refused to let her drive herself after that, his stubbornness so exasperating that it was easier just to go along with him.

Without a glance in her direction, he turned on his side, presenting her with his broad back. Her stomach roiled as he shut her out even further.

It had seemed so innocent a couple of hours ago. She'd been hit hard by the news that one of their students, a promising young man they'd been sure was college-bound, had been arrested for drug trafficking. Jason hadn't betrayed the least emotion when she'd called him at midnight, but he'd been the one to suggest she come over for pizza and beer.

She couldn't stand the silence anymore; she had to say something. The mortification was killing her.

She tightened her grip on the covers. "Jason—"

He pushed away from her and slid from the bed. In the glow of the small bedside lamp, she got one heart-stopping glance at his gorgeous backside before he yanked the bathroom door open and disappeared inside.

Anger bubbled within her at his brush-off. She wanted to march in there after him and give him a shake.

Or she could just leave. This might be her only chance to escape without confronting Jason at all. It didn't seem right to simply ignore what had happened between them, but for once, she was perfectly content to take the coward's way out.

Jumping from the bed, she scrambled through the room, gathering up her skirt and blouse. She found her pantyhose in the kitchen and her sandals in the living room. Within a few minutes, she was dressed and out the door.

As she drove through streets wet with spring rain, she contemplated her next move. Avoid Jason completely the last few months of school? Make light of their lovemaking, as if it hadn't been the most mind-blowing pleasure she'd ever experienced? Or pretend it had never happened?

She'd decide tomorrow, when she saw him again. Let him take the lead. Stone-hearted Jason would likely go with option three. Fine. She could deal with that.

Even if it hurt.

Chapter One

She wanted to see him.

Jason Kerrigan tightened his grip on the wheel of his silver Mercedes as he headed up Interstate 80 toward Reno. Six months with no contact, then out of the blue a letter from Ashley Rand.

Not a letter. Little more than a note: "I need to talk to you," neatly penned, followed by her name, address and phone number.

Surely she didn't want to rehash that night at his apartment in Berkeley—not six months later. It might have been a mistake on a massive scale—never mind how incredible the sex had been—but he figured she'd said it all when she'd walked out without a word.

The tires squealed around another tight curve. He wrestled the car back into his lane as it hit the warning bumps. He'd just passed the town of Marbleville and from the Mercedes's GPS system, he knew the Hart Valley exit was another seven miles ahead.

What could she possibly want? Was she in some kind of financial bind and needed money? She'd never seemed particularly impressed with his wealth, but necessity could be a strong motivator. If it was money she wanted, this would be a short reunion.

He didn't have time for this. He should have pressed her harder to tell him what she wanted over the phone, saved him the six-hour round trip. Maybe she thought he'd have a harder time saying no to a loan face-to-face. Obviously, she'd never sat across the table from him in a business negotiation. Few executives in the high-tech industry relished a confrontation with Kerrigan Technology's youngest CEO.

As a Bay Area native, tiny little backwater towns like Hart Valley weren't exactly his cup of tea. Too many trees, too much dirt and likely everyone stuck their noses in everyone else's private lives. No matter what Ashley had to say, he wouldn't be staying long. He'd brought a change of clothes and his computer—he didn't go anywhere without his laptop—but he intended to finish his business with Ashley this afternoon and get home before his brother's bedtime at nine.

He spotted the sign for Hart Valley and pulled onto the exit ramp. A quick glance at the directions and he turned right, toward town. That much closer to Ashley and clearing up whatever she thought was so important he had to drive 170 miles to hear.

Even slowing to twenty-five, he was through the small town of Hart Valley in less than a minute. Which meant he was less than six minutes away from Ashley's sister's place, according to the GPS.

It was possible she wouldn't be there. He hadn't been able to guarantee he'd drive up this Friday afternoon. "Tentatively," he'd said, then when he'd called her back to confirm, he'd had to leave a message on her cell's voice mail.

So what if she wasn't there? He couldn't see himself sitting around at her home located in the back of beyond waiting for her. But to turn around and return to San José without seeing her didn't seem right, either. He'd committed himself to this visit; he'd follow through.

Stoney Creek Road came up quicker than he expected, and he had to hit the brakes to keep from missing the turn. According to the GPS, 2.2 more miles, then he'd arrive at the NJN Ranch. A knot tightened in his chest.

He slowed as the Mercedes's trip meter counted out 1.8 miles and he watched for the address. This wasn't like the city, with houses crammed side by side, all of them identified clearly with numbers painted on the front. The few addresses he'd seen along Stoney Creek were scrawled haphazardly on scraps of wood or on fence posts. They didn't seem to go in any order, either.

Luckily, the ranch had a large wrought-iron sign over the front entrance, the letters *NJN* prominent enough he couldn't miss it. As he turned onto the gravel drive, creeping along its bumpy surface, he saw a large, covered arena and a barn on the hill beyond it. He parked beside a silver hatchback and shut off the engine.

He glanced at his watch, then checked his PDA for new e-mail. Even in the few hours he'd been gone, it had piled up, just another reminder that this trip to indulge whatever nonsense Ashley had to share with him pulled him away from more important issues. Like whether Kerrigan Technology's recovery from its financial woes would continue or if the mistakes his late father had made would take it under.

Dropping the PDA on the seat, he climbed out of the car and by reflex hit the alarm button on his key chain. Taking a look around him at a vista filled with trees and grazing horses, he unlocked the car again.

There was a small house at the far end of the arena, an odd octagonal structure. As he started across the parking area toward it, a woman emerged from the front door, her face, her movements vaguely familiar. His heart rate accelerated, a knee-jerk response to those white-hot moments six months ago. When he got a better look at the woman, though, he realized it wasn't Ashley after all. Her hair was darker than Ashley's strawberry-blond and she wasn't as slender.

"Can I help you?" She gave him a businesslike smile as she shook his hand. "I'm Sara Delacroix, director of the Rescued Hearts Riding School."

A flicker of motion through the front window of the house distracted him. Was that Ashley?

"Sir?" Sara repeated.

"Sorry." He kept his gaze on that window. "I'm Jason Kerrigan."

Sara moved between him and the house. "What can I do for you?" There was an edge to her tone now.

Irritation welled up in him. "She's expecting me."

"She's my sister." Sara's hazel eyes narrowed. "She never mentioned you were coming."

"Is Ashley here?"

Silence stretched as Sara speared him with her gaze. "Just a minute."

She strode back toward the house and gave the door a peremptory knock before she opened it. Feminine voices drifted toward him, then Sara stepped out and motioned to him. As he walked toward the house, he heard Sara ask, "Do you want me to stay?" then heard a soft no in response.

Sara gave him a dark look as she passed him, and when he glanced at her over his shoulder, she still had her eye on him. He ignored her, starting toward the house.

Sara had left the door slightly ajar, and he started to push it open. He could almost see his long-dead mother wagging a scolding finger at him. Biting back impatience, he knocked and waited.

She had to be just inside, but several seconds dragged by before the door finally moved. When Ashley stepped clear, his world narrowed on that first glimpse of her face.

He'd remembered her as attractive, but her brains had placed her above most of the gorgeous women at school who couldn't resist the allure of his money. What he hadn't recalled was the silkiness of that strawberry-blond hair, how enticing her soft brown eyes were.

Then his gaze drifted down, giving in to the impulse to take in all of her. If her face had sent his imagination racing, his first sight of her body stopped it in its tracks. He understood that what she'd called him up here to discuss was far more complex than money.

Ashley Rand was obviously, noticeably, most certainly pregnant. And if he'd learned any math at all back at Stanford and Berkeley, the baby was his.

* * *

How could she have thought she'd ever be ready to face Jason Kerrigan again? Standing just across her threshold, he looked even more stiff and formal and coldhearted than she remembered back at Berkeley. His neat, gray polo shirt and impeccably creased charcoal slacks screamed boardroom rather than backwoods ranch. No doubt, dirt wouldn't dare come to rest on that pristine fabric.

"Hello," she said, at a loss as to how to muster any other greeting.

He didn't answer, his gaze fixing for a moment on her face before it dropped again to her six-months-pregnant belly. Under his scrutiny, a nausea kicked up that rivaled her eight weeks of morning sickness. She had to resist the urge to shut the door in his face.

His perfect patrician brow furrowed. "We used a condom."

She tried to smile, but her face felt too stiff. "Best-laid plans."

His gaze locked with hers. "Why did it take so damn long to tell me?"

"Everything about that night was a mistake. I wasn't keen to revisit it."

His jaw worked. "I still had a right to know."

She should have called him the moment the test stick turned blue. But sometimes she could hardly believe that night had actually happened, that two near strangers—barely friends—had burned for each other that way. Then, after the ultrasound and Dr. Karpoor's startling news, she'd needed time to wrap her mind around her predicament, time to get past the panic. It had taken her this long to get up the courage to call.

Even now she was reluctant to share the miracle inside her. "How do you know it's yours?"

He didn't even blink. "It's mine."

She dug her heels in at his arrogance. "How can you be sure? I wasn't a virgin."

He fixed her with his dark eyes. "You might as well have been."

While she reeled at that bald assessment, he looked past her into the house. "Can I come in?"

Again the impulse surged inside her to shut the door. If she ignored him, maybe he'd leave, then she could pack everything up in her bug and disappear. She certainly had enough experience disappearing.

But things were different now. She started teaching at Hart Valley Elementary in another week, had a classroom full of second-graders to educate. It was what she'd trained for these past several years at Berkeley. Not to mention Sara and her new baby. How could she leave her sister and nephew behind?

He put a foot up on the threshold. "We need to talk about this, Ashley."

She imagined Jason stepping inside, the small space filled with his presence. Back at Berkeley—until that night—she'd never entertained the least lascivious thought about Jason. But now memories crowded her mind, his skin against hers, his mouth everywhere. The images overwhelmed her. She would be an idiot to allow him into the close quarters of her quirky octagonal house.

She needed a chance to get her head on straight again, to reestablish Jason as the prickly, straitlaced man she recalled from school. Anything else she might be feeling was just hormones and not worth crediting.

Pulling the door shut behind her, she squeezed past him onto the deck of the front porch. "Let's take a walk."

He followed her down the porch steps and toward the pasture and paddocks where the horses dozed. As they passed the tack room, she grabbed the brand-new bucket of treats Sara had left there. Before she'd gone more than a step, Jason plucked it out of her hand. "You shouldn't be carrying anything heavy."

She tried to take it back. "It can't be more than five pounds."

He pulled it out of her reach and read the label. "Five point five."

She would have wrested it from him, but the last thing she needed was a tug-of-war. Giving up the battle, she continued toward the paddocks. He gestured for her to go first when the walkway narrowed around the corner of the covered arena, and she made sure to keep her distance. Up the hill, the horses had noticed their approach and stood at attention in their paddocks.

In early September, the Sierra foothills still shimmered with heat. The grass on the rolling pasture that had glowed a vivid green in the spring lay drooping and yellowed now. September's shorter day was a relief, but at four in the afternoon, sunset was still a few hours away.

They arrived at the first gate to the pasture area. He put a hand out to stop her as she reached for the latch. "How far along?"

She bit back her irritation. "You can count as well as I can."

He pushed open the gate before she could. "Six months, then." He studied her swollen belly. "You're pretty big."

"Thanks for the reminder."

When she reached to shut and latch the gate again, he stood in her way to do it for her. The temptation to give him a poke rose up inside her, but that would mean touching him. She wasn't touching him. "I'm not an invalid, for heaven's sake."

"I know." His gaze moved from her face down the length of her, and despite her swollen body, she felt a trace of heat in the wake of his scrutiny. She'd heard sometimes women were more easily aroused during pregnancy, but she hadn't believed it, until now. Maybe rampant prenatal hormones explained the baffling attraction she felt for him.

Not that he wasn't easy on the eyes. He was as close to beautiful as a man could be, lean but muscular, with high cheekbones and deep brown eyes that had always fascinated her. There were lines bracketing his full mouth that hadn't been there back at school and a new burden on those broad shoulders. She suspected she knew what weighed him down but wanted to see if he'd bring it up on his own.

One of the horses nickered, then the other five joined in. "They're waiting," she said, hand outstretched for the treats.

He pulled them out of reach. "I've got them."

Resolute, she grabbed the handle and tugged, but he wouldn't relinquish the bucket. They might as well have been a couple of two-year-olds fighting over a toy.

"I can carry it," she said through gritted teeth.

With his free hand, he loosened her grip. As she lost

her purchase on the handle, she tried to hold on to her irritation, but his warm touch distracted her. His fingers enfolded hers and his thumb traced one slow circle on her palm. She felt his arm tense as if he intended to pull her closer.

Then one of the horses called again and he dropped her hand. "Sorry." Turning on his heel, he strode toward the paddocks. Her heart hammering, Ashley headed up the hill after him.

Once he had the bucket open, she gathered up a handful of treats and walked along the line of horses. As the white pony neatly lifted a treat from her palm, the question that had been burning inside her worked its way out. "Why didn't you tell me?"

His dark gaze fixed on her. "Tell you what?"

She wanted to pound her fists on his chest. "About your father."

Not a speck of emotion in his face. "What would it have mattered?"

"We were friends."

"We were barely that."

It was true, wasn't it? But it cut so deeply. Especially considering the life growing inside her. "But you just left without a word."

His gaze drifted to the trees beyond the paddocks. "You left first." He said it matter-of-factly.

"I left your bed that night," she conceded. "But you left school."

He pinned her with his gaze, his expression opaque. "I had business to attend to."

"I had to find out in the newspapers that your father died." Shock enough that he had left without a word, doubly painful that he hadn't shared the reason. "If I'd known—"

"What? You might have stayed until morning?"

If she didn't know better, she'd think it mattered to him. But she knew nothing scratched very deeply beneath Jason's surface.

Typical Jason to put her on the defensive. "I needed to think things through. We had one kind of relationship and then…" Their passion that night had completely knocked their casual friendship off its tracks. "I thought I'd have time to find you, to talk to you."

His jaw worked as he looked past her at the pines and cedars beyond the paddocks. "So did I."

When she'd fed the last horse his second share of treats, she brushed her hands off and started back toward the gate. She didn't even bother trying to open and close it herself, just waited for Jason to do it for her. With so much unfinished business prickling between them, she didn't want to add to the tension by fussing over the trivial.

Despite his abrupt departure from school six months ago, she had only to glimpse the rigid determination in his face to realize Jason wouldn't just vanish from her life today. Likely he'd want some kind of resolution in triplicate detailing every iota of his obligation.

What had she expected? She'd called to invite him here, to inform him she was pregnant because she thought he ought to know. He was here, they'd hash out whatever details they had to hash, then he'd leave again. The sooner she got to it, the sooner he'd go.

Ashley forced a smile. "Would you like something to drink?"

"Are we going to talk about this?"

"Of course." Her jaw ached from clenching it.

He returned the treats to the tack room as they passed, then continued on with her toward the house. He paused at the porch steps. "It looked octagonal from the front."

"It was, when Sara lived here." She moved past him toward the front door. "Then her husband, Keith, added the back bedroom."

Ashley had originally planned to make that room the nursery, but after the doctor's bombshell, she'd realized it would be too small. So she'd regretfully given up the larger bedroom, knowing that the nursery would need the bigger space.

Jason followed her into the coolness of the house, his presence as imposing as she'd known it would be. As he took in the comfortable, well-worn sofa and recliner in the living room and the red vinyl chairs and Formica table in the breakfast nook, Ashley edged past him into the small kitchen.

Digging in the refrigerator, she unearthed a can of cola from the back. When she turned to hand it to him, he was right behind her. Her arm brushed against him before she could take a step back.

"Sorry," he said, although he didn't move. If she wanted some space, she'd have to make it herself. But his fingers grazed hers as he took the soda can, and she leaned toward him instead of away.

The pop of the can tab jolted her out of her daze. Sidling past him, she headed for the living room, where she'd left the bottle of water she'd been sipping while she and Sara visited. Her throat felt dry as dust.

Jason followed and stationed himself in the middle of the living room. Not sure what to do next, Ashley took a long swallow of water, then stood with the bottle chilling her hands.

His gaze dropped to her belly. She couldn't blame him. Its size astounded her, too, when she caught a glimpse of herself in the mirror. Not exactly what she'd intended for her first year of teaching.

He lifted his gaze to her face. "Six months, Ashley. Why so long?"

"You disappeared. I couldn't find you."

"You knew how to contact me."

She did. As the young CEO of high-flying Kerrigan Technology, Jason wasn't exactly low profile. "When I found out…I wanted to wait a few weeks, to make sure."

"And then?"

Then she saw the ultrasound. And for a week she could barely think at all. "You left, Jason. I wasn't sure what that meant."

"It didn't mean anything."

"And neither did we, is that it?"

"The reason I left had nothing to do with you and me."

"There was no you and me." She felt faintly ill, but it had nothing to do with morning sickness. "We both know that."

He just stared, jaw taut. "I had to handle my father's estate. Things were complicated."

She waited for more, but it seemed that was all he was willing to reveal. "So where do we go from here?"

He took a drink of his soda. "How long will it take you to pack?"

Of all the questions she might have expected, that wasn't one of them. "Pack?"

"You'll only need enough to tide you over for a week or so. I can send movers to pick up the rest."

A string of memories flooded her mind—Sara coming home in a panic, dragging Ashley along as they packed up everything they owned. Piling it all in the car and racing out into the night, a day away from danger or only an hour.

But those times were over. "I'm not moving anywhere."

"Of course you are. To San José with me."

"No. I live here."

"How else can I take charge of you and the baby?"

She took a breath. "I don't need you taking charge."

His hand tightened on the soda can, bending it slightly. "What the hell does that mean?"

"I can handle this on my own."

He stared at her as if she'd sprouted a second head. "I seem to recall I was in that bed with you."

A startling heat suffused her at the memory—his body over hers, his mouth, his hands touching her everywhere. She chanced a look his way and saw he was remembering, too. His brown eyes darkened, nearly black as his gaze dropped to her mouth.

She suppressed the erotic images. "I'm prepared to take care of everything."

He took a step toward her. "I'm just as responsible for this child as you are."

She should have backed away, but she held her ground. "You don't have to be."

"Of course I do!" Another step closer. "This is *my*

baby just as much as yours. You expect me to turn my back on it?"

"No, I just…"

Somehow his hand was on her arm, his fingers curling around, his thumb stroking. His focus had returned to her mouth, and she was certain if she didn't break that visual contact, he'd kiss her.

She backed out of reach. "You're right. You need to be involved."

"Then you'll come to San José."

"Absolutely not."

He flung his arms out in frustration, sending soda spurting. Slamming the can on a side table, he rounded on her. "My house is twenty times this size. The medical care in the Bay Area is head and shoulders above anything this Podunk town can offer."

She shook her head. "This is my home."

He started to reach for her, then dropped his hands. "Be reasonable, Ashley."

Irritation bubbled up inside her. "I have family here, a job that starts a week from Monday. I'm not uprooting myself for you."

"What about for the baby?"

"We'll be fine here."

"I'm responsible." Raking a hand through his dark-blond hair, he paced away, then turned back toward her. "For both of you."

"I can't leave, Jason."

He paced away again, toward the kitchen and back, agitation tightening his shoulders. So many other men would have been thrilled to be let off the hook so easily, but from the little that Ashley had learned about Jason those months at Berkeley, duty wasn't something he could easily let go.

He confronted her again, determination settling in his face. "Then I'll stay here."

"What?" She shook her head in confusion. "Where?"

"If you won't come to San José—" his hands squeezed briefly into fists, then relaxed "—then I'm staying here, in Hart Valley."

Chapter Two

Would Ashley call his bluff?

She had to know he wouldn't take no for an answer, that he wasn't going anywhere without her. If she believed he'd stay right here, take up residence on her turf, would that be enough to bring her to her senses? Convince her to pack up her things, climb in his Mercedes and return to San José with him?

It sure as hell had better. Because staying here in Small Town, USA, was most certainly not on his agenda. With Kerrigan Technology still struggling out of its financial doldrums, his father's estate still in a mess, he didn't have time to play country boy.

He focused on Ashley, on her delicate face, the lines softened by pregnancy, her belly large with child. His child. His responsibility. He had a duty to protect her and the child she carried, whether she liked it or not. The moment she had stepped from her house, pregnant with his baby, his obligations had extended beyond just his brother, Steven, and his stepmother, Maureen, to encompass Ashley and the life inside her. He couldn't— would never—turn his back on that obligation.

Her gaze narrowed on him. "I'm not leaving."

"I'm not, either."

She tipped up her chin. "Then stay."

Okay, this might take a little time. He made a quick mental assessment of his weekend and decided he might have a day or two of wiggle room in which to work on Ashley. She'd always been a sensible woman, surely she would see reason if he made a clear case to her.

He motioned toward the sofa. "Sit down." He took a breath. "Please."

She eyed him warily, edging around him to the far end of the sofa. When she groped behind her for the sofa arm, he couldn't just stand there and let her flop back onto the cushions. He took her hand to help her down.

The warmth of her skin against his was a shock. Her wide brown eyes locked with his, stirring up memories he'd buried away six months ago. He forced himself to release her, then eased himself into the adjacent armchair.

She rubbed her palms together. "Don't you have a business to run?"

What waited for him at home pressed down on him, but he shrugged as if it didn't matter. "What did you expect, Ashley? That I'd take one look at you and run?"

Color rose in her cheeks. "I didn't think that far ahead."

Obviously, she wasn't thinking now, considering her

adamant insistence on staying. He'd have her convinced by tomorrow.

"How long?" She smoothed her skirt over her rounded belly. A maternity dress shouldn't look so sexy, but there was something about the swirl of colors, her slender hands, that stirred heat inside him.

Heat that hazed his thoughts. "What?"

"For the weekend?"

"We need time to work out the particulars."

Her lips compressed. She didn't like that answer. "You're not staying here."

He looked around at the tiny space, imagined sharing it with Ashley. They'd be shoulder to shoulder, brushing up against each other at every turn, in each other's space. Touching, breathing each other's air.

"No. Of course not." He suppressed his body's reaction. "Where do you suggest?"

"The Hart Valley Inn." As she hooked a strand of silky hair behind her ear, her hand shook. "Pretty much the only place to stay unless you want to go down to Marbleville."

Better to stay as close to her as possible. All the better to keep the pressure on. He needed to tie things up as quickly as he could, get back to San José.

Fate had just wrenched his life into a sharp U-turn, not toward disaster as it had twenty years ago, but toward… something new. Unexpected. He didn't like surprises.

He just needed time to wrap his mind around it, to understand how his world had lurched into unpredictability. He'd learned twenty years ago that if he didn't want the rug pulled out from under him, he'd better keep himself in line, have every detail worked out completely. Otherwise, chaos would sit on his doorstep.

Ashley's brown eyes drew him, tugged at something inside him. Without a mother for so long, he never learned the knack for giving comfort, had never considered it something expected of him. That was a woman's purview. But Ashley's troubled gaze drove him to reach for her.

He folded her hand in his, intending to give her a pat, a smile to ease her. But the moment he touched her, his world shifted again, lust and a baffling longing wrestling inside him.

With the chair and sofa sitting at right angles, his knees nearly brushed hers. The lightweight fabric of her flowery dress shaped her legs, tempting him to run a hand along her still-slender thigh. It might have only been one night, a cataclysmic hour of lovemaking, but he remembered distinctly the feel of her taut skin as he trailed his fingers up to that sweet mystery shrouded in rose-gold curls.

His heart pounded in his ears as he leaned closer, fitting his knee between hers. Balancing on the edge of the chair, he lifted his hand to curl around the back of her neck, threading his fingers into her hair. Her wide brown eyes fixed on him, the heat in them unmistakable. Her lips parted, inviting him in, begging him to brush his mouth against them.

He was near enough to hear her breathing, to catch a trace of her scent. Her inner thigh felt impossibly hot against his leg and an urgency to press her back against the sofa, to cover her body with his exploded inside him.

He let go of her hand, intent on exploring her body. But the terrain had changed, and with the first light contact against her rounded belly, he froze. She's pregnant! What the hell are you doing?

He pushed back, jumping to his feet. "God, I'm sorry."

She just stared at him, looking as stunned as he felt. Color had risen in her cheeks, whether from embarrassment or arousal he didn't want to consider.

"I had no right to touch you."

Her chest rose as she took in a breath. "No, you didn't."

"But my intentions here…" He struggled to frame what he wanted to say. "My only purpose here is to fulfill my obligations. There won't be any other relationship between us."

She tipped up her chin. "Of course not."

Feeling like a complete idiot, he edged toward the door. "I should go. Get myself set up at the inn."

When she started to push to her feet, he motioned her back down. "I'll call you." He shoved open the door and let himself out into the afternoon sunshine.

He didn't let himself think until he'd pulled the Mercedes back onto the road. He had a to-do list a mile long in his PDA, most of which he could take care of with his laptop and a data line. He'd have to call his stepmother, Maureen, and his brother's caretaker, Harold. He'd only brought one change of clothes, so a trip down to that big box store in Marbleville would be in order. Shopping somewhere that didn't stock Gucci and Armani would horrify his stepmother, but he doubted anyone in Hart Valley would notice the lack of designer labels.

Could he reach his attorney this late in the day? He needed a trust fund set up for the baby. Another one for Ashley. Maureen would squawk about that, too.

Should he call his stepmother's butler, have him set up a suite of rooms for Ashley in the mansion? He'd want a place ready for her when he brought her back with him. Preferably in the east wing, opposite his own rooms at the other end of the sprawling Tudor. As far from his as possible.

Like the sweetest fragment of a dream, Ashley's face drifted into his mind. He ought to blot it immediately from his consciousness, but he let it linger as he slowed at the town limits. He hadn't allowed himself to feel even the least anticipation at the prospect of seeing her again. Now something very akin to pleasure threatened to blossom inside him.

Even though she meant nothing to him. She'd been a casual friend at Berkeley, someone he knew wouldn't fit into the life that waited for him outside the university. Their one frantic night of passion hadn't changed that fact.

But the baby did. The baby changed everything. It meant he would have to make a place for Ashley, even if she was nothing more to him than the mother of his child. He could never let her go, not completely. She would always be that one small puzzle piece whose edges never quite matched, whose brilliant colors flamed in the otherwise drab tapestry of his life.

Not five minutes after Jason left, Ashley's cell phone rang. Deep in the sofa's cushions, her body still tingling in the aftermath of what had nearly happened between her and Jason, she stared at the device burbling away on the breakfast counter across the room and considered ignoring its summons.

But it was most likely Sara, and if Ashley didn't answer, Sara would be on her way back here, lickety-split. Ashley had enough on her hands coping with Jason's overbearing presence without Sara complicating matters. Her counselor sister would have her under the microscope, analyzing Ashley's every emotion toward Jason. She'd never believe the short-lived passion of six months ago had burned itself out completely that night.

The phone stopped ringing, but Ashley knew better than to expect Sara would leave it at that. She'd better call her sister back before Sara grabbed her car keys.

With a heave, Ashley pushed up from the sofa and hurried to pick up the phone. It rang again almost immediately. Sara's number flashed on the display.

"Hey, are you psychic?" Ashley smiled as she answered, hoping it would mask the edginess in her voice. "He just left."

"He's the father, isn't he?" Sara rarely minced words.

"Yes." Twenty-three years old and Ashley still felt like a baby sister. "Guilty as charged."

"Why now?" Sara pressed. "All these months since you found out, you'd think he would have turned up before now."

Ashley took a breath. "Until today, he didn't know."

Several seconds of silence ticked away before Sara asked, "And now that he's heard the happy news?"

"He's staying for a couple days. To work things out."

"Staying where? Not with you?"

"Of course not. At the inn."

She could imagine Sara's scowl. "Does he know about—"

"No."

"You have to tell him."

Ashley tried to rub away the tension building between her eyes. "One bombshell at a time."

"What do you know about this man?"

What did she know, other than his connection with Kerrigan Technology? He'd offered so little of himself during their time at Berkeley. Even that night in his arms, when they'd been as physically close as a man and woman could be, he'd kept his deepest secrets secured behind an emotional wall.

"I'm pregnant, Sara. He's the father. I have no choice but to let him be involved."

"Are you going to marry him?"

"What?" The thought twisted her stomach. "Good God, no."

"Because if you barely know him—"

"Marriage is absolutely not an option."

Sara released a long sigh. "You keep me informed. If he takes one wrong step—"

"You'll be the first to know." Ashley said her goodbyes and hung up the phone. She couldn't deal with Sara's mothering right then, not when she needed to work out for herself what to do next.

Sara had protected her for years, first from their abusive father, and later while they lived on their own, a seventeen-year-old and a twelve-year-old fighting to eke out a life for themselves. It was a hard habit for her sister to break and even harder for Sara to accept that Ashley could take care of herself.

The phone still in her hand, she nearly dropped it when it rang again. The caller ID displayed "Kerrigan Technology" on the screen. Her heart rate picked up its pace, but she squelched her reaction as she pressed the answer button. "Hello."

"Do you know how to store a number on your phone?"

The brusque, off-the-wall question was pure Jason. "I can figure it out."

"Save my number. I want to know you can get hold of me if you need me."

But she didn't need him, didn't even want him there. It was very well to tell Sara that Jason deserved to be part of his baby's life, quite another to accept him into hers. The dance they'd engaged in at the university, the steps a mix of respect, mutual interest and occasional awkwardness, had never quite matured into actual friendship. Their night of intimacy had destroyed even that possibility.

"I'll save it. Thanks." She couldn't hold back the most obvious question. "What are we doing, Jason? What comes next?"

"How about dinner?"

"I have work to do. As I'm sure you do."

"Afterward—"

"I go to bed early."

He let out an exasperated sigh. "Then let me take you to breakfast. There's some kind of coffee shop across the street from here."

"Nina's Café. But I can't do breakfast. I'm still getting my classroom set up."

"I'll come with you. We'll talk."

The last thing she wanted was him in her classroom, entangled even further in her life. He didn't belong there. But what choice did she have?

Tiredness swept over her and she realized she simply

didn't have the energy to resist him. "Pick me up at nine."

"I'll bring breakfast." A beep sounded in the background. "I've got a message coming in I've been waiting for."

"I'll see you tomorrow, then."

"I have to take it."

"Okay."

Still he hung on; she could hear him breathing into the phone. "We'll work it out, Ashley." Finally he disconnected.

She stared at the phone, stunned. He'd actually sounded halfway human. Of course, Jason's idea of working things out would doubtless involve him demanding and her acquiescing.

Setting aside the cell, she returned to the sofa to lie down. Exhaustion had been one constant during her pregnancy, made even worse by the extra burden on her body. As she lifted her feet onto the sofa arm and tucked pillows under her head, she considered how she would deliver the rest of the news to Jason. What if that was the tipping point that sent him running? Would that be better than having to grapple with the discomfort his presence stirred up inside her?

She'd prepared herself to do this on her own. How would she fit Jason into the picture? Her father had shown her the ugliness of men, the horror they could inflict on women. Jason would never raise a hand to her, but he was so reserved, so cold, she couldn't imagine him letting her get very close. And what kind of father would such an aloof man be to his children?

He'd been anything but icy that night. She still wasn't

sure how it had happened. If not for the life growing inside her, she could almost believe the fire and passion six months ago had been a dream.

She couldn't think about it now. The exhaustion had seeped even deeper, driving thought from her mind. The faintest rustling in her belly a comfort, she surrendered to sleep.

Jason stabbed the disconnect button on his cell and resisted the urge to slam the device on his desk. He'd expected the conversation with his stepmother, Maureen, to be difficult; he hadn't anticipated such a nasty confrontation.

Usually, he just ignored his stepmother's diatribes. But when she started in on Ashley, it was all he could do to keep his temper in check, to keep from roaring out at the injustice as he had as a child. All those years of careful self-control nearly went out the window. So he'd held his tongue as Maureen played every card in her deck of accusation and condemnation, calling him an idiot for falling prey to Ashley six months ago, and his decision to accept her child as complete insanity. She accused Ashley of using the baby as a ploy to force him to marry her so she could get her hands on the Kerrigan money. His repeated assurance that marriage most definitely wasn't in the cards barely appeased his stepmother.

She'd insisted he demand a DNA test the moment the baby was born. Ranted that by acknowledging the child without any empirical proof was further confirmation of his father's error in placing Kerrigan Technology into his son's hands. He would drive the company into the ground, destroy his father's life's work.

His father had nearly done that on his own with a few bad decisions not long before the heart attack that killed him. His acquisitions of a struggling digital media company and a moribund Internet-based data storage firm had nearly broken the company's back.

He ran his fingers lightly over the keyboard of his laptop. A half-dozen high-priority e-mails awaited his immediate response. A security report required his input, as did a stack of résumés from applicants for a VP of marketing position. He had plenty to occupy himself with tonight.

But with Ashley so close, he couldn't seem to think straight. It made no sense, when he'd barely given her a second thought since he'd left Berkeley.

That wasn't entirely honest. Sometimes, during strategy sessions with Kerrigan's Marketing Department or the interminable discussions with his father's estate lawyer, she'd drift into the periphery of his consciousness. Sometimes it would just be her face in his mind's eye, sometimes that one incredible night of pleasure would unroll like a movie, obliterating any other thought.

Those images invaded now, drumming through him, scents and sensations as real as if she sat beside him. He grabbed the bottled water on the table beside his laptop and gulped down half of it. Dumping it on his head would have been more effective.

He felt so antsy in the small, overdecorated room, the prospect of waiting until tomorrow morning to see her again seemed unbearable. Especially with the specter of his interaction with Maureen still fresh in his mind. He wanted to stand in the same space as Ashley, breathe in the scent of her skin, let the silk of her hair stroke his palm.

He was half out of his chair, hand on his car keys before he stopped himself. Dropping the keys on the small table he'd made into his desk, he forced himself to sit, to focus on his computer.

He tapped at the keyboard until his hands were stiff and his neck ached. Ashley's face kept floating up like a screensaver on the laptop, her sweet smile, her soft brown gaze fixed on him. Likely, whatever he'd typed in those e-mails he'd sent over the last few hours would be unreadable garble and he'd end up sending them all over again tomorrow.

When his stomach rumbled, he was shocked to see it was nearly eight o'clock. He rose, tried to stretch out the kinks in his back. As small as it was, the room was the largest the inn had to offer, with a queen-size bed wedged between two side tables, an armoire and the worktable squeezed in at the other end. It wasn't a business suite by any stretch of the imagination, although some might call its frilly touches homey.

Not like any home he'd ever lived in, though. The Kerrigan mansion had been furnished by a professional interior designer, each piece chosen to suit Maureen's taste. Every room seemed staged, with just the right painting on the wall precisely placed above outrageously priced antiques. The house might as well be a museum.

And yet…there was a memory, buried away, of a different place, a tiny cottage north of San Francisco, its rooms packed with mismatched furniture, its walls crammed with pictures. He'd been five when Kerrigan Technology had taken off, when they'd moved to the mansion. In the three years before his mother died, she'd never quite put her touch on that expansive Tudor in San José.

He pushed up the window fronting Main Street to let in the cool evening air. Hart Valley had just about rolled up its sidewalks for the night, nearly every storefront dark. Only Nina's Café across the street was still open, but the last car parked out front pulled away as he watched.

Thank God he was only staying a day or two. He was used to the vibrancy of San José and San Francisco. This sleepy little town unsettled him, gave him too much quiet space. The high tension of the Bay Area suited him better, kept his mind active, distracted him from the darkness that always edged his life.

Headlights approaching from the other direction caught his attention. The car, an old-style VW bug, slipped into the parking slot next to his. A woman stepped from the car, the dim light from the Hart Valley Inn sign revealing the gold-red color of her hair. Ashley. She was here.

His heart thundered at breakneck speed, and he gripped the windowsill as she lifted her gaze to the inn's second floor. She found his window, although it wasn't the only one lit. The VW's door still open, she stood there, frozen. She looked ready to climb back into the car.

Don't go! The sound of his own voice rang in his ears, and he realized he'd said it out loud. In the preternatural silence of Main Street, she had to have heard. Still she clung to the car as if planning her escape.

Finally she slammed the door shut and started for the inn's front door. Relief surged through him. It alarmed him that her arrival meant so much to him, and he clamped down on the emotions that threatened to bubble up.

Backing from the window, he looked around the room and realized how hazardous it would be to have her here, especially after their close call in her living room. He'd catch her downstairs before she came up. They could meet down in the parlor where the inn hosts set up coffee in the morning.

By the time he stepped out onto the landing, Ashley had already reached the bottom of the stairs. Her beauty stunned him momentarily, so she'd climbed several steps before he could speak.

"I'll come down," he told her, starting toward her.

Gripping the rail, she hesitated. "I have to talk to you."

He stopped on the step above hers. "You'd better not be here to tell me to leave."

"I'm not," she said, tension edging her tone.

"We can't go to my room."

Heat flared in her eyes. "No. We can't."

He edged past her, putting out a hand. "We'll sit downstairs."

He might as well have been offering her a snake instead of his hand, but she took it. The way she leaned on him as they descended the last few steps told him she needed his help more than she would likely admit.

She let go the moment they reached the bottom, but he held on long enough to guide her toward the parlor. "Is that normal?"

Hands lightly on her belly, she glanced at him sidelong. "What?"

"You're exhausted." He took her hand again to help her down onto the sofa in the parlor.

"Why wouldn't I be?" She leaned her head against the unforgiving high back of the Queen Anne sofa. "It's late."

"It's eight-thirty." He sat beside her, keeping a decorous two feet between them. "At Berkeley we'd stay up all night arguing economic theories."

She smiled, looking his way. "You argued economic theories. I lectured you on Shakespeare."

Her eyes were half-lidded from tiredness, he realized, but he could so easily picture that red-gold head on a soft pillow, bedroom eyes beckoning him. "What did you want?"

Her gaze slid away. "There's something I have to tell you."

His heart pounded as irrational fear surged through him. "There's something wrong with the baby."

Startled, she turned back to him. "No. The babies are fine."

His thought processes ground to a halt. Babies? He struggled to put two and two together, to come up with—

"Twins, Jason," she said, her expression serious. "I'm having twins."

Chapter Three

Jason pushed off the sofa so fast Ashley thought he would run the moment he gained his feet. But he only stood staring at her, the emotions in his face baffling. The shock she understood. But the flicker of sorrow didn't make sense.

He strode across the inn's parlor, restless as he'd been at her house. Beth Henley, the inn's owner, had filled the small room with an eclectic mix of thrif3t shop and antique furniture, so there wasn't much clearance for pacing. Six feet out, six feet back, Jason threatened to wear out the old-fashioned rag rug.

"You're sure?" he asked.

"Of course. The doctor detected the second heartbeat at eight weeks."

"And they're both fine?" He flexed his hands as he stood over her.

"They're perfect."

"Do you know…"

"From the ultrasound, it looks like a boy and a girl."

His eyes shut a moment. "Not identical, then."

"No." She wondered why that seemed significant to him.

He resumed his trek back and forth across the rug. "That decides it, then. You're coming to San José."

If her feet weren't throbbing and her energy level near zero, she would have jumped up and throttled him. "I'm staying here, Jason. I already told you that."

"You need to be under a physician's care."

"I've been seeing Dr. Karpoor right in town."

"But if anything went wrong—"

"The hospital is twenty minutes away. They can life-flight me to Sacramento if necessary. I've got it covered."

He seemed to stuff away his agitation, his face smoothing to neutrality. "We'll discuss it later. When you're not so tired."

She would have told him there was nothing more to discuss, but her weariness had her at a disadvantage. "I'd better get back." She pushed against the sofa's stiff cushions.

He closed his hand around her elbow and eased her up. "I'll take you home."

The warmth of his hand drifted up her arm, tempting her to lean into him. "I have my own car."

"You're worn out. You shouldn't be driving."

She shook off his hand, not liking how vulnerable she was to his touch. "I'll be fine. It's only a few miles."

He was ready to push the issue; she saw him mustering his arguments. He'd been on the debate team as an undergrad at Stanford. She imagined he'd been a ruthless competitor.

"Call me when you get home. Did you save my number?"

"Not yet."

"I'll do it."

He put out an imperious hand. She would have walked away, but he'd come after her. Far easier to just hand the cell over to him.

With characteristic focus, he tapped the appropriate keys on the phone, then gave it back to her. "I set up a speed dial. Just press five."

He walked her out to her car, opening the door for her and taking her hand to help her swing her bulky body inside. He didn't let go, bending down to eye level.

He stroked the back of her hand with his thumb. "I can't let anything happen to them."

"Of course not."

"Tell me you'll be careful." His gaze drilled into her.

"I will. Of course."

He stared at her a moment more, then backed away, shutting the car door. He stepped up onto the sidewalk in front of the inn, but he waited while she started the VW and backed it out of the parking slot. She caught a glimpse of him still standing on the sidewalk in her rearview mirror just before she turned off Main Street.

He was a man with so many sharp edges, she didn't know how she would tolerate him over the next couple of days. She'd been bossed by her sister, Sara, for years, but she'd accepted that because Sara supported them both and had to make the decisions. But Sara had gladly snipped the apron strings years ago and rarely played the big-sister card anymore. Jason's orders rankled her.

But it was only for the weekend. Then he'd return to San José and likely their contact with each other would be limited. They'd probably have to make some kind of custody arrangement once the babies were born—a prospect that filled her with anxiety—but surely he wouldn't want the day-to-day responsibility of raising children. It made more sense for the babies to live here. He could visit them whenever he wanted. She doubted that would be often.

As she pulled into the gate of the NJN ranch, her heart ached at the thought. While she was growing up, she would have given anything for a real father—a good man, a kind and decent man who would come watch her soccer games and school plays. Her classmates would moan and groan about their dads, how restrictive they were, how they wouldn't let them do anything. Those same girls would be dragging their dads around on back-to-school night, showing off their artwork and science projects.

Unlocking the front door, Ashley stepped inside the quiet, empty space. She loved the little house, its tidy efficiency, its quirky lines. She'd felt comfortable here the moment she'd arrived three months ago.

But as she slipped off her sandals and padded toward her bedroom in the back, an aching loneliness washed over her. Before Jason arrived, she'd been happy in her solitary life, willing to accept motherhood on her own with the assistance of her sister and friends she'd made

in Hart Valley. But Jason seemed to represent possibilities she'd made an effort to block from her mind—an
intact family, a complete home.

She couldn't let herself think about it even now.
Because Jason would be gone soon, back to his own
world. He'd likely try to force financial support on her,
would no doubt set up trust funds for the twins. He
would offer her nothing emotionally. He didn't seem to
have the capacity for it.

Pulling on a short frilly nightgown her sister had
given her, Ashley climbed between the pale-pink sheets
of her double bed. She'd had to give up the queen-size
bed when she gave up the larger room to the babies. She
didn't need the bigger mattress anyway, living alone.

As she lay there, eyes closed, she tried to imagine
Jason in the bed beside her. His serious face as he gazed
down at her, stroking her cheek, pressing a kiss on her
lips. His hand resting on her belly, waiting for the twins
to kick. His arms cradling her all night long.

But that man didn't really exist. Jason was only a few
miles away in Hart Valley, but the real core of him
might as well be in a different universe. He'd no more
hold her to ease her loneliness than he would give away
his millions and become a monk.

One night she'd seen more, she'd delved deeper into
his soul. As much as she might want to tell herself it was
only lust the night they'd made love, there had been a
moment, just before passion overwhelmed him, when
all the barriers had come down. It had been only an
instant, then the walls had slammed into place again.

And that barricade would never fall again.

* * *

What the hell was wrong with him?

He'd tossed and turned half the night entertaining entirely inappropriate fantasies of Ashley before falling into restless sleep riddled with X-rated dreams. Now he sat beside her in his Mercedes obsessing over how her bare, freckled shoulders would feel under his fingers. As bad as the distraction of her soft skin was, her scent, like cinnamon-spiced flowers, completely obliterated his focus.

Oblivious to the irrationality inside him, Ashley flipped through a workbook in her lap, her strawberry-blond hair half concealing her face. She'd made it clear from the moment she opened her door to him this morning that physical contact would not be on the agenda today. Not that he would indulge in his ridiculous fantasies.

He'd barely managed to convince her to take his more-spacious Mercedes instead of her cramped little bug. He couldn't see himself riding beside her in the tiny car, nearly close enough for his shoulder to brush hers. His sedan's bucket seats at least gave him a fighting chance of resisting the pull between them.

The box of pastries he'd so carefully selected at Archer's Bakery in town sat on the floor behind his seat. She'd thanked him for bringing them, but said she still felt a little shaky in the mornings and the rich pastries might not go down well. He obviously knew nothing about catering to pregnant women.

He pulled into the parking lot of Hart Valley Elementary. Moving quickly to her side of the car, he helped her out. "I'll go back into town and pick you up some-thing. What do you want?"

"I have a box of granola bars in the room, and I brought a banana." She slipped the workbook into the large canvas bag she'd brought. "I don't need anything else."

"Some juice? Milk?"

"Thanks, no." She opened the back door and bent to retrieve the box he'd carried out of the house for her.

He stepped in to take it himself. "I'll get it." Arms wrapped around the box, he shut the car door with his hip. When she started to sling the canvas bag over her shoulder, he snagged it, too, and dropped it on top of the box.

She glared at him. "I'm not helpless."

"Where to?"

With a huff of impatience, she started off across a thick green lawn that fronted the school, past the brick-fronted school office to the asphalt playground beyond. Rows of classrooms bordered three sides of the play-ground, and bright-white chalk delineated a baseball diamond in a green field beyond. The September-morn-ing coolness still lingered, although low eighties had been forecast.

For a woman six months pregnant with twins, she walked remarkably fast. She held her shoulders stiffly, the small purse she had tucked under her arm squeezed tight against her side.

They reached the farthest row of classrooms, and he followed her up the ramp that led to the door. Diving in her purse for a set of keys, she fumbled with the lock.

He set the box down and reached for the keys. "Give them to me."

She yanked them away. "I can do it." She fished

through the ring, then jabbed a key in the lock. It wouldn't turn.

"Ashley—" He put his hand out again for the keys.

"No!" Her fingers wrapped tight around the jangling ring. "I'll do it!"

But she just stood there, her soft mouth in a tight line, her fingers woven in the metal keys. He'd caused this; he'd made her angry without even knowing why or how. A typical blunder for him. He could suss out the deepest buried intentions of a business opponent, but when it came to women, he was a stumbling bull.

She fished through the keys again. The one she selected fit in the lock and turned. Her hand on the knob, she pushed open the door, but blocked his way into the room. "I don't want you here, Jason. I know you're the babies' father, that you deserve to be involved. But I wish you'd stayed in San José."

"I'm not leaving," he told her flatly. "Not without you."

"I have a life here. A good one. For me and the babies."

He struggled to hold on to his patience. "Let me inside. I'll help you with your classroom."

The sheen of tears in her eyes shocked him. "I can't have you here."

"We have to come to some kind of agreement."

She rubbed her eyes before a tear could fall. "I know. We have to talk."

She had to know he couldn't just walk away. "Let me inside."

She stood frozen a moment more, then she relented, stepping inside the classroom and leaving the door open. Hefting the box again, he entered, shutting the door behind him.

An eclectic selection of posters were already tacked to the wall, of dolphins and tall redwoods and celebrities encouraging the children to read. Tables arranged in a *U,* two chairs at each, surrounded a carpet filled with cartoon characters.

There was a tear in the carpet, and the tables were stained with ink and paint. The bookcases that lined the walls were riddled with nicks and gouges. Nothing like the private schools where he'd been educated, where everything was bright and new, always in perfect condition.

One phone call and he could get Ashley a job at any of the most exclusive private schools in the Bay Area. How could she pass up such tantalizing bait? He considered making the proposition, but as upset as she was, she might not be as receptive as she could be. He tucked that idea away as he set the box on the table nearest her desk.

"What grade are you teaching?" he asked.

"Second. I have nineteen students."

"What can I do?" he asked.

He thought she might ask him again to get out of her life. But instead, her gaze narrowed on him. "Leaves." Her mouth curved in a faint smile. "I need 150 of them."

Uncomprehending, he shook his head. "Leaves."

Behind her, construction paper lay in stacks on top of a low bookshelf. She gathered up a sheaf of red, orange and brown paper and dumped it on the table near her desk. Setting a leaf-shaped pattern, a pencil and a pair of scissors beside the construction paper, she pulled out one of the minuscule chairs.

"Leaves. Fifty in each color. There's plenty more paper if you need it."

He hadn't played with paper and scissors since... maybe he never had. All those exclusive private schools stuck to the academic basics, training the next generation of tycoons. There was little room in the curriculum for arts and crafts.

As he wedged himself into the tiny chair and slid a sheet of orange construction paper over, he glanced at Ashley, now unloading the canvas bag and box. Her gaze locked with his, and the faint curve of her mouth widened to a genuine smile. "If you do well with the leaves, I'll promote you to tree trunks."

Her smile set off an ache inside him he didn't understand. Something about her soft brown eyes, the way the sunshine spilling in from the wall of windows turned her silky hair to gold made him feel...lonely.

He pushed aside the useless emotion. "A hundred and fifty leaves," he said, picking up the scissors, "coming up."

As she flipped through the workbook she'd brought and wrote out lesson plans at her desk, Ashley indulged in another surreptitious glance over at Jason as he worked. A twinge of guilt started up inside her again that she'd given him such endless, mindless duty to keep him busy.

It hadn't been revenge so much as self-defense. He'd unsettled her from the moment he'd arrived at her door this morning in his snug red polo and crisp navy slacks. There wasn't anything suggestive about what he wore; he was the picture of the hard-driving CEO, a bit intimidating, a lot exasperating. It was his dark-blond hair—

so impeccably neat it begged to be mussed. Her fingers itched to rearrange it.

Lack of sleep and crazed hormones sent her mind wandering in such dangerous directions. She truly didn't want to know how that red knit would feel under her hand, what she'd see in his eyes if she touched him. So she used his trick—aloof coolness, putting as high a wall around herself as he did around his emotions.

But watching him with the scissors and construction paper, that blond hair still in desperate need of mussing, she knew she couldn't hold up barriers against him for very long. She just didn't have his knack of keeping people at arm's length.

His angular body might not fit well in the mini-size chair, knees nearly to his chin, broad shoulders towering over the chair back, but he seemed surprisingly at home tracing and cutting out leaves Ashley's students would be using their first week of class. He focused on the activity as he did everything else—single-mindedly and with precision, as if his company's bottom line depended on the completion of the task.

Some men might have considered such a trivial chore beneath them. He hadn't complained, hadn't argued, had just sat down to do it.

Her stomach rumbled, and she realized she never had gotten around to eating that banana. When she'd refused Jason's offer of breakfast, she hadn't been completely honest. While her body didn't always respond well to rich food, even in her sixth month, she wouldn't have said no to a pastry from Archer's Bakery if her sister had bought it for her. It was harder to accept Jason's generosity.

But her stomach's call for sustenance trumped her

misgivings over the significance of Jason's gesture. Something buttery and sweet from that pink bakery box would be absolute heaven.

"Jason."

He looked up at her, setting aside the scissors and flexing his hands. "Ten more to do in brown and orange."

"I'd be glad to finish them if you'll go get the pastries."

The tiny chair tipped over as he rose, and he righted it before straightening. He winced as he stretched his shoulders back.

Ashley pushed to her feet. "I'm sorry. I never should have had you sit in that chair."

He squeezed the back of his neck with his long fingers. "Just a little stiff."

"Come sit here." She gestured to her cushioned desk chair. "I'll get the kinks out for you."

Dropping his hand, he took a half step back. "No."

She should let it go. He was always tense, and the occasional neck rubs she'd given him at Berkeley had never made much of a difference. It was something she'd always done for Sara, to ease some of her sister's stress. When she'd massaged Jason's tight muscles at the end of a long day at the university, it had been just as innocent.

Until that fiery night in his arms. Now nothing between them seemed innocent anymore.

Despite her better judgment, she pulled her wheeled chair out and beckoned him. "Come here."

He moved toward her with slow steps and settled in the chair. Resting her hands on his shoulders, she ran her thumbs along the tense muscles there. His heat radiated through the knit of his shirt.

Her heart rate kicked into high gear as she worked her fingers toward the strong column of his neck. He sucked in a breath when she first touched bare skin. "Are my hands cold?"

He shook his head. Trying to ignore the sensual awareness that sparked deep inside her, she dug deep with her fingertips on either side of his neck. The tautness of his muscles persisted against her ministrations, as if he resisted even the slightest bit of comfort she offered. Back at school she could usually cajole him into a modicum of relaxation with her gentle massages. Today she suspected nothing would persuade him to let go.

Except a kiss. A shock went through her at the thought of pressing her lips to the side of his neck, feeling the warm flesh against her mouth. She wondered at his reaction, whether he'd push her away or turn the chair to pull her into his lap.

She realized her deep massage had changed, that she'd begun stroking his neck instead, grazing his skin in sensual caresses. She could hear his harsh breathing, feel arousal coiling under her hands. It crossed her mind she should pull her hands away, cease touching him. But the sensation of skin against skin had her mesmerized.

His hands fell on hers, stopping her. His shoulders rose and fell, his muscles, if anything, tighter than when she'd started. Then he pulled away, pushing the chair aside, facing her.

His fingers curved around her upper arms, and he held her there, not pulling her closer but not pushing her away, either. His gaze dropped to her mouth, and the expectation that he might kiss her sent a fever through her.

But then he stumbled back, breaking the contact. He strode toward the door, yanking it open and slamming it behind him.

Dazed, Ashley made her way to the chair where Jason had been working, and eased herself into it. A mistake, she realized the moment she stretched her legs out under the equally small-scale table. She'd have to struggle to get herself back up without help.

But Jason would come back, wouldn't he? They'd settled nothing about the babies, hadn't even started to discuss it. He wouldn't leave now.

Thirty minutes later she'd cut out the last of the construction-paper autumn leaves when she heard the rattle of the door opening. Jason stepped inside with the pink bakery box and a brown paper bag in his hands, hesitating in the doorway before he crossed the room toward her.

He set his burdens down and opened the box for her. "I remembered you like bear claws."

There were four of her favorite pastries in the box, lined up beside two cheese and two raspberry danishes. She laughed. "I'm as big as a house as it is. Are you trying to fatten me up even more?"

"You need to eat." He handed her a bear claw, then took a raspberry danish for himself.

She took a bite of the sweet, buttery pastry, sighing with pleasure. Sitting on the edge of the table, Jason leaned forward and brushed at the corner of her mouth. "Some sugar," he said, his voice low.

The pressure of his thumb lingered. Ashley resisted the temptation to lick the spot he'd touched, to see if she could taste him. "There are paper towels back there by the sink. Could you get us a couple?"

Setting the danish on the box lid, he went for the paper towels. He set one sheet on the table in front of her and another in her lap. He did nothing out of line as he spread the towel over her legs, but she imagined his touch nonetheless.

"Orange juice or milk?" He opened the brown paper bag and pulled out a small carton of each.

He'd gone back into town after all. "Milk would be great."

He opened the carton for her and took the juice for himself. "You finished the leaves. Thanks."

"I should be thanking you. They're for my students."

"But I said I'd do it. It was my responsibility to finish the job."

Was everything a responsibility, a duty? She wondered if he ever did anything for the sheer pleasure of it, then remembered their night together.

Once she'd polished off the bear claw and milk, she wiped her face and stuffed the paper towels into the milk carton. He took her trash before she could so much as stir, then returned to where she still sat trapped in the diminutive chair.

"What next?" he asked.

"Decorate the room," she told him, then she smiled. "That is, after you lever me out of this chair."

He frowned, giving her his hand. He let go the moment she was on her feet. "Where's your cell?"

"In the canvas bag."

Moving to her desk, he grabbed the bag and dug

through it. Ashley was too stunned to complain at his intrusion.

He unearthed the phone and brought it to her. "Keep it handy."

She slipped it into the pocket of her sundress. "What—"

"I want to make sure you can reach me while I'm gone. It'll take me an hour or two to get everything arranged."

Wariness rose inside her. "Get what arranged?"

"What I need in order to conduct business. Office equipment, communications system. Some clothes. A place to stay long-term."

The unease within her blossomed into full-blown alarm. "I don't understand."

"You need me here, Ashley, and not just for a couple days." His brown gaze bored into her. "If you won't come with me to San José, I'm here for the duration. Until the babies are born."

Chapter Four

Jason's departing footsteps still echoing in her ears, Ashley nearly sank back into the tiny, second-grader chair before she caught herself. Jason staying? Until the babies were born? She'd be stark raving mad before those three months were up.

Bending to the knee-high table, she gathered up the stacks of paper leaves and sorted them into manila envelopes. She would unpack the box of books she'd brought, then turn her focus on decorating her room. Best to put aside the problem of Jason for the moment. Fretting over what he might or might not do wouldn't be good for the babies.

Nearly two hours later she'd finished stapling up an elaborate paper oak tree that covered one wall, intending to add leaves decorated by the students the first week of school. A few die-cut squirrels hid amongst the branches and a great gray owl she'd cut from a poster watched over the scene.

Glancing at the clock, she saw it was nearly one and her stomach started clamoring for food again. Jason had left the box of pastries, but it would be tempting fate if she ate another bear claw. There was still the banana and granola bars, but her insistent appetite wanted something more substantial.

She crossed the room and stepped outside into the simmering late-summer heat. A few other rooms had their doors propped open, so she wasn't alone here. She could see the principal's car in the parking lot, but Mrs. Beeber wasn't the type to socialize with staff, so Ashley wasn't inclined to invite her out to lunch.

Slipping her hands in the pockets of her sundress, she fingered the phone, dithering over whether to call Jason or just wait. Her imperious stomach wasn't in a patient mood, so she tugged out the cell and tried to remember which preset Jason had used to store his number.

Before she could dial, the sun's glare off an arriving car flashed across her face. She watched as Jason's silver-gray Mercedes pulled in next to Principal Beeber's Volvo. Her hand tightened on the phone, and the cell beeped as she inadvertently pressed a button. She realized she'd speed-dialed Sara's number and she quickly poked the disconnect.

Jason had started across the playground, the heat off the asphalt shimmering across his body. He was drop-dead gorgeous, there was no denying it. Couple that with the fact that she knew what he looked like under those straitlaced clothes, and it made sense that she responded to him the way she did. It didn't mean anything more than pure animal lust, even in a woman six months pregnant.

Halfway across the playground, she could feel his gaze lock on her. The late-summer sunshine couldn't compete with the impact of Jason's dark-brown eyes. She wrapped her hands around the safety railing on the landing, doing her best to ignore a new kind of hunger burning inside.

She smiled, hoping it didn't look as come-hither as it felt. "I hope you're taking me to lunch."

He started up the ramp. "We can do that first."

She got to the door before him and stepped back into the air-conditioned classroom. "Before what?"

"We get your things packed."

About to pick up her purse and the canvas bag, she turned to face him. "Are we back to this? I'm not going to San José with you."

"Not San José. I'm leasing a house in town. We'll move you in there."

Just as well she'd already put those books away. Otherwise she'd be heaving a few at his head. "I'm staying in my own house."

He had the pink bakery box in his hands, and the pressure of his thumbs dented the lid. "I don't like you living out in the middle of nowhere alone."

"My sister's in and out of there all the time. Once school starts, I'll be here every day."

She could almost hear his mind working. Tension set off an ache in her back. Nothing was ever easy with Jason.

The box under one arm, he plucked the canvas bag from her desk. "We'll talk about it later," he said as he walked toward the door to wait for her.

* * *

Jason remained silent during the short drive into town, no doubt marshaling additional arguments to convince her. Ravenous hunger battling with her habitual afternoon exhaustion, Ashley wasn't sure she could face another round with him.

The lunch crowd at Nina's Café had already thinned by the time she and Jason stepped inside. There was only Nina sitting at a table with her son, Nate. Nate sketched on an art pad with a concentration unusual for a six-year-old.

"Hi, Nina," Ashley called out. "Hello, Nate."

Rising, Nina welcomed Ashley with a smile and gave Jason a curious glance. "Go ahead and sit anywhere."

His hand lightly brushing her back, Jason urged Ashley toward the table next to Nate's. As Jason seated Ashley, Nina brought them two menus before hurrying to answer the café's phone. Jason turned to study Nate's riotous pastel of flowers and giant bumble bees.

"Can I take a closer look?" he asked the boy.

His expression as serious as Jason's, Nate handed him the sketch pad. Jason held the artwork up to the light. Ashley expected he'd inform Nate that the bees were too big or that real flowers didn't come in that shade of lime green. But he surprised her.

He set the pad back down on the table. "You're very good."

Nate grinned. "Thanks."

"My brother likes to draw."

That bit of personal information startled Ashley. She had no idea he had a brother.

"Is he as old as me?" Nate asked. "I'm six."

Jason's jaw worked. "He's older than you."

He turned away from Nate abruptly and sat beside Ashley. "What's good here?" he asked, picking up the menu.

She suspected if she asked about his brother, he wouldn't be forthcoming. "Everything. I like the hot meat loaf sandwich."

Nina returned to take their order, and Ashley could see the questions in her eyes. Ashley's sister was no gossip, but Sara and Nina were good friends. It wouldn't be long before the café owner knew everything there was to know about Jason Kerrigan and why he was here.

Not ten seconds after Nina brought Ashley's clam chowder and a basket of crackers, Jason started in. "The property I've leased has a guest cottage, where I'll be staying. You'll have the main house to yourself."

She took a bite of soup. "I have a house, Jason."

He just rolled on. "The previous tenants set up one room as a nursery. You'll sleep in the adjoining bedroom."

Exasperated, she set down her spoon with a clatter. "Are you going to choose the color of my sheets, too?"

Sheets made her think of beds, which led her mind to bodies in that bed, limbs entwined, skin against skin. His gaze fixed on her mouth, sending a spreading heat through her. She snatched a packet of crackers, her hands shaking as she tore them open.

"I'll leave that to you." His chair scraped as he shifted backward. "The house is just up the street—a few doors down from your doctor, and only a half mile from the school. You can walk anywhere you need to in town."

Picking up her spoon, she waved it at him. "Are you through?"

"I've arranged a truck to move your things today."

She stared at him, his arrogance striking her speechless. Throwing the spoon at him wouldn't be very ladylike, so she took another bite of soup. At least she could quiet her empty maw of a stomach.

Nina's arrival with their lunch bought her more time. Ashley waited until the café owner had returned to the kitchen for their rolls before she spoke.

"You cannot waltz in here and run my life," she said, pitching her voice low.

"I'm just doing what makes sense. Pregnancy is difficult enough for a woman—"

Frustration put an edge in her voice. "You don't strike me as someone who's had much contact with expectant women."

A bite of gravy-laden meat loaf halfway to his mouth, he flicked a glance at her. "Just one."

Something about the way he said the quiet words tugged at her heart. But empathy was a dangerous emotion where Jason was concerned. "I'm not moving," she said wearily for what seemed the hundredth time.

He chewed the mouthful with slow deliberation, then set the fork on his plate. She remembered back at the university when he'd sat down with one of the at-risk kids who had threatened to drop out of school to work in the family business. Jason had sat the young man down and worn him out with one reasoned argument after another.

Would he do the same to her? She was too tired to argue. The temptation to just get up and walk out nearly had her on her feet.

He must have sensed her desire to escape, because he laid his hand on hers. "Please," he said.

She didn't want to meet his gaze, was afraid of what she'd see there. When she lifted her eyes to his, her heart squeezed tight in her chest. The pain was well hidden, buried so deep she shouldn't have been able to see it. But as old as it was, it must have been profound for that trace to still linger in his eyes, the lines of his face.

"Please," he said again, the pain completely masked by his polite, neutral tone.

She couldn't possibly say yes. But how was she going to tell him no?

He saw her answer in her eyes even before she shook her head. He scrambled for another persuasion, another argument he could use to sway her. He considered resorting to the kind of hardball tactics he'd seen his father use with a balky business opponent. But the thought of belittling Ashley, tearing into her the way his father had, made him feel sick inside.

He wasn't even sure why it seemed so crucial she move to the house he'd leased. Maybe because if she took that step, he'd find it easier to convince her to take the next—returning to San José with him. Or maybe because having her nearby was the best way to keep her and the babies safe.

He didn't know why he was holding her hand, either. It sure as hell didn't fit the businesslike relationship he'd envisioned between them. In the past twenty-four hours with Ashley, he'd blindly followed one impulse after another, something he hadn't done since he was a reckless eight-year-old. Over time, he'd learned to appreciate instinct, but he thoroughly vetted those mental lightning strikes before taking even a single step in the direction they pointed.

Close contact with Ashley seemed to drive reason from his brain. He pulled his hand free, hoping it would clear his mind. But he just wanted to touch her again.

Picking up his fork, he took another bite of gravy-soaked mashed potatoes. "Come see the house."

She shook her head again. "It won't make a diff—"

"Come see it. If you still say no…" But he wouldn't let her. He'd find a way to make her say yes.

She shrugged. "I'll look at the house."

They finished their meal in silence, Ashley's brow furrowed as she ate every bite of her turkey sandwich and French fries. He felt her gaze on him occasionally; when he glanced at her sidelong, he could see her soft mouth compressed with irritation. She didn't like being pushed, but pushing was what he did best. It didn't usually bother him—applying pressure on a reluctant client was a part of doing business. But guilt niggled at him using that tactic with Ashley.

She waited for him by the Mercedes while he paid the check. He only gave half his attention to the café owner as she rang up the sale, too concerned Ashley might walk off without him.

"So you're the one," Nina said as she gave him his change.

He fumbled the quarters she'd handed him and they clattered on the counter. "Excuse me?"

"The father." Nina retrieved the coins, dropped them in his palm again. "So, are you going to marry her?"

A faint glimmer of a memory tugged at him—his mother catching him in a lie about eating cookies before supper. For a moment, he felt like that little boy again. "It's none of your concern."

To his surprise, she laughed. "If you can find a way to keep the Hart Valley busybodies from nosing into your affairs, I want to hear about it. I never figured that one out." She smiled lovingly at her son, still working at his drawings.

Jason pocketed his change and left the café. Ashley leaned against his sedan, her hands interlaced on her rounded belly.

"We can walk," he told her, gesturing across the street. The refurbished Victorian was half-hidden by pine and oak trees.

When she pushed off from the car, she swayed, putting her hand on the roof for balance. He moved to her side and took her arm. She didn't object as he walked beside her across Main Street.

Another old memory flickered—holding his mother's hand, his brother on the other side. His mother's belly as rounded as Ashley's.

Clamping down on the image, he helped her up onto the sidewalk. "There's a stairway on the other side of the creek."

As they cut through the public parking lot beside the Hart Valley Inn, they passed a small frame house nestled against the creek. A curtain twitched aside, and he glimpsed a face in the window, dark eyes following their progress.

"Whose house is that?" he asked Ashley as they crossed the wooden bridge spanning the creek.

As Ashley looked over her shoulder at the house, the curtain dropped. "Arlene Gibbons." Ashley sighed. "I guess we've given the town busybodies something to chew over at breakfast tomorrow morning."

"It's none of their business."

Ashley laughed. "You're not in San José anymore."

On the other side of the bridge, a short dirt path led to the foot of the stairs. Ashley's mouth curved in a wry smile as she gazed up at the myriad steps built into the steep hillside. "Is this an evil plot to force me to exercise more?"

What was he thinking? "I'll get the car." He turned back toward the bridge.

"I can manage." She chuckled softly. "It'll be good for me."

He went behind her, ready to offer support if she needed it. But other than stopping to catch her breath on a landing halfway up, she made her way steadily to the top.

The stairs led to the curving driveway of the Victorian. Catching her breath again, Ashley took in the pillared front porch. A second-floor balcony served as the porch roof.

"It's lovely," she said, her eyes softening.

To him it was just a house—the only one in town immediately available. The previous tenants had moved due to an unexpected job transfer. The guest cottage tucked into the rear of the lot was an unexpected bonus that had made it feasible for him to move Ashley here.

As she walked toward the porch, he tried to see the place through her eyes. Time had faded the cornflower-blue paint and broken and chipped some of the white gingerbread trim. During his brief visit earlier today, he'd discovered a cracked window on the second floor and had demanded the property management company replace it. If the interior hadn't been in excellent condition, he would have looked elsewhere for housing.

From the top of the steps, Ashley turned to him. "Can we go inside?"

He joined her on the porch, pulling the ring of keys from his pocket. Between the weathered wooden park bench and the withered pots of flowers, there wasn't much room for both of them to stand. That is, if he wanted to avoid brushing against her.

As he slipped the key into the lock, he could feel her just behind him, everything about her soft and feminine— her hair, her skin, her scent. He wanted to abandon his efforts with the key and turn to her, put his arms around her. The bougainvillea shrouding the sides of the porch secluded them from view; no one would see him kiss her.

Twisting the key, he unlocked the door and shoved it open. Stepping aside to be sure he put plenty of distance between him and Ashley, he gestured her inside.

"Oh," she murmured, turning to look around at the living room.

It seemed an ordinary room to him, filled with antique sofas, chairs and side tables, with a glass-fronted cabinet against one wall and a hat tree by the door. He'd learned enough about antiques from his stepmother's endless rounds of decorating to know the ones populating the Victorian's living room weren't particularly valuable, although they looked more comfortable than the stiff-backed monstrosities Maureen had chosen for the Kerrigan mansion.

The real attraction in the room stood right in front

of him. Light spilling in from the windows turned Ashley's silky hair to spun gold, touched her cheeks with peach. The gentle smile on her face set off an ache inside him.

He shook off the unwelcome feeling. "It was built the turn of the last century. It's probably drafty as hell in the winter."

She headed for the kitchen just off the living room and he followed. Thankfully this room had been updated somewhat, a fairly late-model dishwasher, stove and refrigerator installed. The cabinets had been freshly painted, but the hardwood floor looked original, its surface refinished but scarred with a century of use. Ashley seemed just as enamored of the plain white cabinets and tile countertops as she'd been of the unremarkable living room.

It was like that in the rest of the house, as well. The dining room with its nicked sideboard and long dark table and chairs, the sunporch in the back with its tired wicker chairs and bench, the brilliant-green lawn rimmed with weedy flowers, bisected by the path leading to the cottage. She even exclaimed over the carved handrail along the stairs to the second floor, her fingers passing over the worn spots as if those were its best feature.

The upstairs at least had undergone some major reconstruction. Five tiny rooms had been converted to three, a third bathroom added to the one upstairs and one downstairs. The bedroom he took Ashley to first, the master suite adjacent to the nursery, was an acceptable size, twice as large as either of the original two rooms that comprised it. Unlike the downstairs, the bedrooms weren't furnished.

"I'll need to bring my own bed and dresser," she said, walking across the floral-patterned rug.

"I'll buy you new," he told her. "You ought to have at least some decent furniture in this house."

"What I've got is fine." He heard the irritation in her voice. "I just bought them."

He doubted they were of any quality at all, doubtless purchased at the big box store in Marbleville. While he considered how he would order some good, solid pieces for her and have them delivered, the import of what she'd said hit home.

"Then you'll stay." The rush of emotion inside him he chose to identify as relief.

She laughed, her expression rueful. "I think I have to."

Of course she did, but it surprised him that she realized it. "It's best for you and the babies."

Her expression sobered. "That remains to be seen. Let me show you something."

She opened the purse she'd been carrying through-out their tour, tugging out her wallet. Zipping it open, she pulled out a ragged square of paper from a small inner pocket. She unfolded the paper carefully, then held it out to him.

It was a color picture torn from a magazine or news-paper. Lines crisscrossed the image where it had been folded, but he could make out the photograph of a house. A Victorian, blue with white trim. Not an exact twin to the one he'd leased, but near enough to send a chill up his spine.

He handed back the picture. "I don't understand."

"I tore that picture from a magazine fifteen years ago. It was my dream house, the one I swore I'd live in some day." She refolded the paper with exquisite care and tucked it back in her wallet. "It looks like you've given it to me."

Chapter Five

Jason would have sent a crew of men to her house that afternoon to pack up everything she owned and truck it over to the house. But Ashley stood her ground on one point at least—she needed the weekend to get herself organized and ready for the move. She wanted time to determine what she should bring with her and what she could leave behind. If nothing else, the extra couple of days would allow her to get accustomed to the idea before he uprooted her.

Fate dealt a hand in her favor in the form of a pay-roll-system crash at Kerrigan. When Jason balked at leaving her she nearly hogtied him and dragged him to his Mercedes. She desperately needed time to herself.

He gave her the keys to the house just before he left Saturday evening. Wiped out by the turn of events,

Ashley collapsed into bed at nine o'clock, deciding to wait until Sunday morning to call her sister. It would be easier to face World War III after a good night's sleep.

When Ashley called after breakfast, Sara informed her the moment she picked up, "I'm coming over," then hung up.

Ashley waited for Sara by the covered arena, and marched over to her sister's sedan before Sara could turn off the engine. Opening the passenger door, she jangled the house keys. "Let me show you the house." She slid into the car, smiling over her seat at her infant nephew, Evan, in the back before she strapped on her seat belt.

Sara scowled at her. "You can't seriously intend to live with this guy."

Ashley laughed, hoping it would ease the knots in her stomach. "Even by Hart Valley standards, this sets a record for gossip exchange."

"Arlene Gibbons called Beth Henley at the Hart Valley Inn, Beth called Nina at the café, Nina called her husband, Jameson, at home, Jameson called Keith at the ranch while he was feeding this morning and I got an earful over breakfast."

Ashley fussed with her seat belt, rearranging it over her belly. "How is your husband?"

"Mad as hell and ready to tear into Mr. Kerrigan. Then we hear from Beth that Jason cleared out last night."

"He'll be back tomorrow." She wasn't sure what she wished more—that he wouldn't keep his promise...or that he would.

Sara pulled into town and turned left at the Stop-and-Go. Ashley looked over at her sister as they climbed the steep grade of the driveway, wanting to see her reaction when she saw the place.

She wasn't disappointed. When Sara stopped the car at the top of the driveway, she smiled and turned to Ashley. "It's your house."

The warmth she'd felt yesterday seeing the place for the first time filled her. "Wait until you see the nursery."

Once Sara had strapped Evan into his baby carrier, Ashley took her sister inside and through the first-floor rooms. The narrow kitchen with its dated tile work inspired Ashley with its possibilities. The wall between the service porch and kitchen could come down, opening up the space, the tile replaced with granite and the cabinets stripped of paint.

As she dreamed, Ashley felt Sara's narrowed gaze on her. "You know it isn't really your house."

"It's the closest I'll ever come to the fantasy." Ashley turned a wistful smile toward Sara. "Don't spoil it with reality."

Sara held her tongue as Ashley led her up the stairs. Ashley opened the door to the master bedroom first, crossing the worn rug to show her sister the backyard view from the windows.

Her arms cradling Evan in his carrier, Sara peered out across the verdant green lawn. "So, he's staying out there."

"We'll have to share our meals. The guest cottage doesn't have a kitchen."

Turning, Sara fixed Ashley with a stare. "You barely know the man. How can you do this?"

Ashley folded her arms over her swollen middle. "He's not going to go away."

"That doesn't mean you have to live with him." Sara closed the space between them, her hazel eyes on Ashley's face. "Are you in love with him?"

The preposterous notion shocked her into silence for a moment. Sara's eyes widened, and Ashley realized her sister had interpreted the hesitation as a yes.

"No!" Ashley said firmly. "Good grief, no. I barely like him."

"But you slept with him." She gave Ashley's belly a pointed look.

"That was…" She struggled to find an explanation for something she didn't understand herself. "We were both lost that night. Something drove us…but not love."

"And there's nothing going on between you now."

Heat rose in Ashley's cheeks. "I'm six months pregnant."

Sara quirked a brow. "I've been pregnant, Ash. It didn't slow me and Keith down."

Ashley tried not to let the close calls between her and Jason show in her face. "Our relationship is strictly platonic." She barely believed herself.

Another moment of scrutiny, then Sara nodded. Whether in acceptance or to put off the discussion for the moment, Ashley didn't know. She took Sara's hand.

"Let me show you the nursery." She led her toward the connecting door.

Again Ashley watched eagerly for her sister's reaction. Sara's face softened with a smile as she took in the nursery walls. They'd been painted in bright colors with jungle animals—curious monkeys, birds with brilliant plumage, secretive jaguars. The sunshine spilling in from the windows dappled the jungle greenery with light. The rug on the hardwood floor continued the motif, featuring a roadmap through thick verdant forest.

"This is marvelous," Sara said, genuine admiration in her voice.

"Plenty of room for the twins."

Sara speared her with her gaze. "Where are you going with him, Ashley? You tell me you don't feel anything for him, and yet—"

"I don't know." Ashley rubbed her belly, wishing she could soothe her own misgivings. "We made a mistake six months ago. And now…honestly, when this is all settled, I doubt he'll be much in the babies' lives."

"He leased a house," Sara pointed out. "He's staying until they're born."

"But he can't stay forever." Ashley shook her head, denying the possibility. "I refused to go with him to San José. This is his way of getting some kind of control of the situation. He doesn't like the unexpected, the unpredictable."

Sara took Ashley's hands. "But one minute you're happy living at the ranch and the next he's got you moving here. Why would you do this?"

Ashley gazed around the room, taking in the jewel colors of the parrots and toucans, the amber eyes of the jaguar. "This is my house. I want this to be the babies' home."

"You can't afford the rent on your own. What happens when he leaves?"

An ache settled in Ashley's chest. "Then I'll go back to the ranch. But at least the twins will start here. And maybe someday…"

Sara let it go, her expression still troubled, but she seemed to understand. Ashley didn't tell her sister the rest of it—that a small softness had settled inside her, a somewhat reluctant gratitude that Jason had given her this house, even temporarily. That thankfulness didn't really mean anything at all; there was no point in mentioning it to Sara.

They picked up sandwiches at the deli in town and headed back to the ranch. Halfway there, Evan decided he'd been quiet long enough and started wailing, requiring Sara to feed her hungry son before she could have her own lunch. Ashley wolfed down her turkey sub, then held the baby while Sara ate.

After lunch, while Evan slept, Sara drove into town for empty cardboard boxes that Nina had put aside at the café. Ashley and her sister spent the rest of the afternoon packing. They'd nearly emptied the kitchen and the bathroom and had most of the linens boxed when Sara finally collapsed on the sofa to nurse Evan again.

Ashley helped Sara feed the horses, then walked her out to her car. As Ashley gave Evan a goodbye smooch, Sara turned in her seat. "Anytime, day or night…if you need me, you call."

"I will."

"If you want me to come get you, I will. I'll move you back to the ranch, send Jason packing."

Ashley reached across the car to squeeze her sister's hand. "I know."

She backed away and shut the door before Sara could say anything else. Then she turned toward the house.

Her cell phone started jangling the moment she

opened the door. Her stomach somersaulted when she realized it was Jason.

She pressed the answer button, had barely raised the phone to her ear when he barked out, "Where were you?"

If she could have reached through the phone, she would have given him a poke. "Keep talking to me that way, Jason, and I'm hanging up the phone."

Silence ticked away, then he released a long exhalation. "I'll be there in an hour. I'll pick you up for dinner."

"Did it occur to you I might have plans?"

"Do you?"

She shut her eyes and struggled for patience. "I don't work for you, Jason. I don't have to do what you want just because you demand it."

More silence. She wondered if his cell phone had lost reception on a mountain curve. Finally he asked, "Would you have dinner with me?" his tone stiff and formal.

Her irritation subsided. "I'll be ready at seven."

"I'll be there at six-thirty."

"I won't answer the door until seven."

She hung up the phone and set it aside. She had an hour and a half to shower and catch a quick nap. She'd need all the rest she could get before Jason arrived.

They went into Marbleville for dinner, to an Italian place Sara had recommended. As they walked into Vincenzo's, the restaurant was packed, tables pushed together to accommodate large families, parents and grandparents riding herd on a multitude of children.

Harried mothers smiled at Ashley as she and Jason

threaded through the obstacle course of tables, a grand-mother calling out, "When are you due?"

When she answered, they clucked over how large she was, then beamed when she informed them she was carrying twins. A phalanx of little ones patted her tummy, fascination in their innocent gazes, their expressions so sweet, Ashley yearned for the day she'd hold her own two in her arms.

When Jason seated her at the small corner table, she saw the tension in him, beyond his usual edginess. She waited until one of the larger tables cleared out and the noise level in the restaurant quieted.

"How was your trip?"

His face set, he took a sip of water. "Fine."

With a huff of impatience, Ashley covered his hand with hers. "We're spending the next three months together, you might as well let me in on your world a little bit."

His hand lay rigid. "There's nothing you can do."

"Remember at school, when you'd talk through a problem with me?" She squeezed the back of his hand. "So, talk to me."

He stared down at the table, then turned his hand until he wrapped his fingers around hers. "Do you know how important you are?" He lifted his gaze. "You are everything to these babies."

His intensity sent a shiver through her. "They mean everything to me."

"While I was in San José, I signed a trust over to you. No matter what happens, you and the babies will have everything you need."

"That wasn't necessary."

"Of course it was. They're my children." His thumb stroked the back of her hand restlessly. "I have to protect you."

Abruptly, he let go of her hand. Taking another sip of water, he launched into a discussion of the two low-performing companies his father had acquired before he'd died. During the rest of dinner, they brainstormed alternatives to laying off the two hundred employees displaced by the merger. Although the tension never quite left him, it eased. But the memory of Jason's earlier intensity lingered.

Jason sat behind the workstation he'd had delivered early Monday morning, his gaze on the view out the front window of the guest cottage. He'd spent all of Monday and part of Tuesday setting up his office in the cottage's front room, figuring he could keep an eye on the main house that way. He hadn't considered how dis-tracting it would be continually watching over Ashley.

She hadn't let him call the movers to bring over her belongings, had barely let him help at all. Her sister and brother-in-law had arrived at the ranch Monday morn-ing with their pickup truck and a handful of friends. He'd had to wait for the delivery of his own furniture, and by the time he drove over to the ranch, they'd carried nearly everything to trucks and cars. There'd been nothing left for him to do.

He'd initially scheduled a conference call for this morning to hash out some of the options he and Ashley had come up with to preserve the maximum number of jobs after the merger. But with two or three key players unavailable until this afternoon, he'd had to push the meeting to after lunch to allow everyone involved to be present. With his notes already typed up, he could spend the morning working through the myriad other tasks competing for his attention.

Except he couldn't seem to take his focus off the house. He'd seen little of Ashley since Sunday night when they'd lingered over dinner tossing ideas back and forth, the rapid-fire conversation reminding him of the one bright spot of his time at Berkeley.

Yesterday, Ashley and her family and friends had turned the chore of moving into almost a party, shouting and joking with one another, sharing sodas from a cooler the café owner and her husband had brought. In the three short months Ashley had lived in Hart Valley, it seemed she'd made more friends than he'd made in a lifetime. Of course, friends mattered far more to Ashley than they did to him. Still, he marveled at how quickly she'd come to fit in.

At lunchtime, she came out to the cottage to let him know her brother-in-law had picked up pizza at the deli in town. He went over to the house, but felt so out of place with the garrulous crowd, he took his slices and returned to the cottage. Later he'd turned down their dinner invitation, instead going back into Marbleville alone for another meal at Vincenzo's. But without Ashley there, the excellent food had lost its savor.

He'd walked over to the bakery this morning, picking up a cheese danish for himself and two bear claws for Ashley. He'd intended to take them to her, to make sure she ate breakfast.

He had the back door unlocked and had been about to go inside when he remembered their exchange

Sunday on the phone. "I don't have to do what you want just because you demand it." He'd locked the door again and returned to his cottage. The bear claws still sat in the pink box on the file cabinet.

He could call her. It was nearly ten; she must be awake by now. Even if she'd already eaten breakfast, they had matters to discuss—his access to the house, for instance. They'd already agreed he would use the kitchen, but did that mean he would enter whenever he felt the need?

He picked up his cell, stabbed the speed dial for Ashley's phone. It rang four times, five. The voice mail picked up. He disconnected without leaving a message, on his feet and tossing the phone aside in one motion.

As he strode across the lawn, he considered the possibilities. She might still be asleep and didn't hear the ring. She could be in the shower. Before it could fully form, he shut down the image that thought generated—Ashley naked and soapy under the shower spray.

Or she could have hurt herself and couldn't get to the phone. A slip in the shower, a fall down the stairs… She could be lying somewhere unconscious, unprotected.

He took the last few yards at a near run, shoving the key into the lock and twisting the knob hard. The back door opened onto the service porch and he had to dodge the wash sink and the hot water heater to slap open the swinging door to the kitchen.

Frantic now, it took him a moment to register Ashley at the stove, her hand on the teakettle as she turned to face him. The shock of seeing her, whole and unhurt, a soft fluttery sundress flowing around her ripe body, stopped him in his tracks. With a quick scan he took in her freckled shoulders, sun-kissed arms, bare feet.

He'd never considered feet particularly erotic. But Ashley's, slender and perfect, the arch delicately curved, her ankles fine-boned, sent his mind spiraling off in crazy directions.

He backed up a step. "You didn't answer your phone."

Lifting the teakettle, she poured hot water into a cup beside the stove. "It's on my nightstand. I wasn't about to race up the stairs to get it."

"I needed to reach you."

She swished her teabag in her cup, the motions of her hand jerky. "I would have checked the message in a minute."

Anger simmered in the aftermath of his fear. "You should have had it with you."

She took a breath as if to answer, then pressed her lips together. Throwing away the teabag, she stirred honey into the cup, took a taste, added more honey. She set the cup on the small kitchen table, pulled out a chair and sat.

Sipping her tea, she pulled a newspaper across the table toward her. When he realized she intended to ignore him, he tugged out a chair and sat next to her. "We have to discuss this."

She took another leisurely swallow of tea, her tongue flicking out to swipe the corner of her mouth. A dim memory surfaced of his own tongue exploring there, then diving inside to taste her.

When she finally raised her soft brown eyes to meet his, she must have seen the memory playing across his face. Her cheeks flushed, the pink even more tantalizing than the motion of her tongue.

She focused back on her tea. "I'll try to remember to keep the phone with me."

He caught the scent of cinnamon, maybe from the tea, maybe from her silky hair. He edged his chair back. "The house has phone jacks installed. I'll set up a land line for you."

Alarm widened her eyes. "No."

"I'll call today. We'll get it activated—"

"No!"

"There are probably jacks upstairs and down, so I can reach you when I—"

"I can't have a phone!" She pushed back from the table, rattling the tea cup.

He'd upset her again, pushed her too hard or in the wrong direction. He had no idea what transgression he'd committed this time. "Why not?"

She took a breath, edging her chair to the table again. "I have my cell. I don't need a land line."

"I say you do."

Her hands trembling, she picked up her tea. She didn't drink, just stared down into the cup. The silence stretched for several moments, then she lifted her gaze to his. "Go ahead, then. But put it in your name."

"I'll pay for it, Ashley, whether it's in your name or mine."

"Just don't put my name on the account."

She was still unhappy, he could see that much. Frightened of something he didn't understand. He had no idea how to fix it, and frustration nibbled at him.

He turned his attention on something he could fix. "Did you eat?"

Her brow furrowed. "No. Just the tea."

He rose. "Don't move."

He hurried out of the house and to the cottage,

grabbing the pink box. For once, she'd listened to him and still sat at the table. Sliding the box onto the table, he opened cupboards until he found a plate and set it in front of her.

She gazed at the bear claw he served up with a bemused smile. "Trying to fatten me up even more?"

"You like them."

"Yes, but…" She reached across the table and squeezed his arm. "Thank you."

Her words, the soft curve of her lips warmed him. He didn't know what to do with the unfamiliar emotion, didn't know how to respond to her. Turning on his heel, he left the kitchen and returned to his cottage to work.

Chapter Six

After Jason left, Ashley couldn't manage much more than a few bites of the bear claw he'd brought her. The rush of panic over the telephone had made her restless, and the familiar urge to run closed in on her. To stave off the impulse to pack up her car and escape, she instead drove over to the school to work a bit more on her classroom. If she kept busy, maybe she could let go of the fear.

There wasn't much more to do to prep for her first day, so she poured her energies into cleaning—wiping the tables, asking the janitor to bring over his vacuum, dusting the bookshelves and organizing the books. She worked through the lunch hour, then realized she was ravenous. Picking up a sandwich at the deli, she ate nearly half of it as she drove home.

After letting herself into the house, she made a

beeline for the kitchen where she unceremoniously dumped her purse and the sandwich. Grabbing a glass of milk, she polished off the rest of her lunch, sitting back with relief when she'd finished. A whimsical image popped into her mind—the babies side by side in her womb, wolfing down twin sub sandwiches.

After throwing away her trash and rinsing her glass, she wandered to the dining-room windows overlooking the backyard. Seeing Jason there, working in the cottage, calmed her, soothed the wildness he'd riled up just a few hours ago. In his bull-in-a-china-shop way, he'd only been trying to make things easier for her. He'd had no idea the potential for danger in having her name included in a telephone directory.

But he's dead, she reminded herself. He can't possibly be a danger to you anymore.

Yet despite Sara's assurance that their father was long dead and buried, Ashley couldn't seem to let herself believe it. The man still haunted her dreams, even though Sara had been his main target and suffered the worst of his rages. He'd only hit Ashley once, and Sara had hustled them both out of there that same night.

But Sara didn't know about the vague images that sometimes invaded Ashley's mind. In the years since her mother's death, she'd decided what seemed like memories must only be part of a dimly recalled nightmare, a horror stitched together from the reality of her father's abuse of her sister. Ashley was only five when her mother died, a five-year-old girl with a vivid imagination.

The glass fronting the guest cottage was rippled with age, blurring Jason's face. The lid of his laptop obscured his broad chest, his wide shoulders barely visible on either side. He wore a crisp black polo inscribed with a small Kerrigan Technology logo and gray slacks; she remembered how crisp the crease had been when he came into the kitchen this morning.

He looked up and caught sight of her. Closing the lid of his laptop, he rose and headed for the cottage front door. When he emerged, he carried a big black garbage bag.

He crossed the yard to the back door and knocked. She would have expected him to let himself in as he had earlier.

She hurried to the door and pulled it open. "Come on in."

He stepped past her, lugging the bag. "We need some rules."

She followed him into the kitchen. "What's in the bag?"

"One of your friends brought it by." He swung it up onto the kitchen table. "Do I knock before I come in? Am I only allowed certain hours? We should have worked this out before now."

Ashley reached for the twist tie on the bag. "If you need to come in for something to eat, just use your key. If you have to come over after nine or ten in the evening, I'd rather you called first."

"That's acceptable. Except…" He raked his hand through his hair. "I don't want to…invade your privacy."

The twist tie wouldn't give way and she considered tearing the bag open. "I'm assuming you won't be barging into my room."

"But if you were downstairs, I wouldn't want to… catch you unawares."

She turned to him, puzzled a moment. Then the lightbulb came on. He was afraid he'd catch her undressed. The thought of him walking in on her should have made her uncomfortable. Instead it sent an erotic thrill down her spine.

Suppressing the sensation, she yanked off the twist tie and tugged open the bag. She smiled with delight at her first glimpse of the contents. "Baby clothes."

She held up the tiniest shirt she'd ever seen. "Who brought these?"

"The woman from the inn."

"Beth. These can't all be her kids' clothes."

"She said she collected them for you." He stepped closer and took a desultory look at the bag. "I can buy you new. You don't have to take hand-me-downs."

"But these are barely used." Ashley dug deeper and unearthed a darling striped sleeper. "And they're from my friends. That makes them special."

He stared at her as if the concept of friends was foreign to him. But maybe it was. At the university, he didn't seem to spend time with anyone besides her and the kids they tutored. She often saw him alone on campus.

"Can you take these to the service porch? I'll get them washed."

He helped her load the washer, then after extracting a promise from her that she wouldn't carry the large load upstairs herself, he returned to the cottage. It took two very full loads to wash everything in the large bag, and she was glad she'd already bought a gentle detergent. The second load wouldn't fit in the laundry basket, so she left it in the dryer.

Eager to get the clothes upstairs and put them away in the babies' dressers, she went out to the cottage. The door was open, letting in the late-summer sunshine. On the phone, Jason motioned her inside.

She stepped into the small front room, reluctant to venture too far into his personal space. He had his back to her, his entire focus on his phone conversation. The black polo shirt he wore clung to his body like a second skin, the dark knit molding to his taut muscles. The temptation to move closer, to try to ease the constant tension in him, tugged at her.

Barking out a goodbye, he slammed the phone into its cradle. Ashley edged nearer. "Problem at work?"

He shot from his chair and wrapped his hands around her upper arms. "The babies are mine."

The intensity of his declaration startled Ashley. "Are you asking?"

"Yes." He shook his head. "No, damn it. I know they're mine. Why do I let her—" His jaw flexed as he cut off the words. "You needed something."

His hands had gentled on her arms, stroking down their length. He seemed distracted, as if unaware of what he was doing.

"The laundry," she said, with not quite enough breath.

His hands moved up again, gliding along her skin, until they cupped her shoulders. His gaze dropped to her mouth.

Her lips parted and she wet them with her tongue. She hadn't intended it as an invitation, but every part of her seemed impossibly aware, ultrasensitive. She couldn't bear the thought of him backing away without at least giving her one taste.

He didn't disappoint her. Leaning close, his mouth brushed against hers, just the lightest touch. When she tipped her head back, he kissed her again, the pressure exquisite. The third time, his tongue slipped along the seam of her lips, not asking for entry as much as exploring their texture.

One hand moved lower to rest along the side of her rounded belly. "Mine," he said softly, with a fierce possessiveness.

He meant the babies, but a small part of her wished he meant her, as well. That there was more between them than one crazy night, that the two of them and these babies meant a family. But that was only her old, hopeless dreams.

She knew there was a bedroom in his small cottage, and she entertained a fleeting fantasy of him taking her there. They could fall into his bed as they had six months ago, enjoy each other's body, each other's touch. It wouldn't mean anything more than it did then, but maybe she could burn away the sensual awareness that seemed to always sparkle along her skin when he was near.

He pressed his body closer to hers, fitting her against him as close as he could. He lifted his hand higher, to the lower curve of her breast, made heavy by the pregnancy. As he sipped at her mouth, tasted with his tongue, his thumb stroked the underside of her breast, leaving it aching.

She felt the hard ridge of him against her hip, and the memories exploded—Jason pulling her silk blouse over her head, unzipping her skirt with shaking hands. Both of them naked on the bed, his hand urging her legs apart.

His thumb nearly grazed her nipple, and she moaned with the anticipated sensation. He thrust against her, a hand on the small of her back holding her tight. She thought she'd explode with excitement.

Abruptly he stiffened, backing away out of reach. He stared at her, his breathing harsh, the heat burning in his eyes. Then he fumbled behind him for his chair and sank into it. "Have to get back to work."

She nearly made her own escape when her clouded mind recalled the reason she'd come out here. "I'm ready to take the clothes upstairs." The breathless words seemed inane.

With his gaze fixed on his laptop screen, he shifted in his chair. "Give me a minute."

She could guess what had him restless in his chair, what he needed that minute for. Arousal still clung to her own skin as she retraced her path across the lawn. She'd never felt such a powerful desire for a man, had never even felt it for Jason until that night with him. Afterward, when he'd left the university, she'd done everything she could to suppress her memories of the experience.

Somehow it had all come roaring back.

Once in the house, she headed straight for the downstairs bathroom, turning the cold water faucet on full blast. Cupping water in her hands, she splashed her face, hoping to lave away the heat that still lingered.

Reaching for a towel, she studied her dripping face in the mirror. Her lips looked swollen, her cheeks flushed. Maybe it was the pregnancy. Maybe it had made her so acutely aware of her body that Jason's proximity was enough to rouse her.

But she'd felt no response to the two young men her brother-in-law, Keith, had brought along yesterday to help with the move. Wyatt and Josh worked for Keith's Delacroix Construction firm, both of them muscular and tanned from daily hard labor outdoors. Lacey, the young waitress from Nina's Café, was fluttering all over Wyatt, but the good-looking carpenters didn't stir even an iota of interest in Ashley.

She heard the back door open and shut. She didn't want him looking for her, so she scrubbed her face dry and stepped from the bathroom. As she crossed the living room, she called out, "Jason?"

The clothes basket in his hands, he stood in the doorway between the service porch and kitchen. "Is this all of them?"

"There's another load in the dryer." She led the way upstairs.

A tendril of connection seemed to tug him up the stairs after her, elevating her awareness of him even more. When she passed her bedroom, she couldn't seem to keep at bay images of leading him into the room, taking him to her bed.

They continued on to the nursery and he set the basket in the middle of the room. "What about the rest?"

The only furniture in the room were the matching dressers Sara had bought for her. They'd intended to go out shopping for the cribs sometime in the next month.

Even though she'd thoroughly vacuumed it yesterday, she wasn't about to put the clean clothes on the floor while he gathered the rest in the basket. "Let me get these put away, then I'll come get you."

He didn't move. "You shouldn't be doing this by yourself."

The aftermath of their encounter in the cottage,

coupled with her usual afternoon lassitude, weighed on her. As tired as she was, she wanted to get the work done. And she was loath to let him coddle her.

"I can handle it."

"Call one of your friends."

"Everyone's working today." Ashley bent to pull a frilly dress from the pile. "Sara had to juggle the riding school schedule to help me move yesterday. I can't ask her again."

Still his feet remained rooted to the carpet. "I have my own work to do."

"Then go." She waved the dress at him. "Do it."

He stared down at the basket of clothes. To her surprise, he reached into the jumble of baby things and pulled out a blue newborn shirt, the garment incredibly small in his large hand. As he held it, what she saw in his face surprised her—reluctance and yearning mixed with old grief. He held himself so tightly, she wondered if he was even aware of the emotions inside him.

It would be best if he went back to his own work, left her to do this job alone. But that ancient sadness pulled at her.

"I'd appreciate your help."

She was sure he'd tell her no, that he'd finally walk out. But he slid the basket closer to the dressers.

He held out the tiny blue shirt. "Where does it go?"

He might as well be holding her heart. Ashley swallowed back her own burgeoning emotion. "Let's assume that's for a boy. We'll do boy clothes in the left-hand dresser, girl clothes in the right."

They didn't speak much as they folded and put away.

Occasionally Jason would ask if a particular item was for a boy or girl; once when he was clumsy about folding something, she demonstrated for him how it should be done. He didn't take offense at her correction, instead watching her with single-minded focus so he could do it right the next time.

The work went quickly. They had both basket loads put away in less than an hour.

Leaning against the girl dresser with a sigh, Ashley rested her hands on her belly. "It's nap time for me. If these two will cooperate."

His brow furrowed. "What's wrong?"

"They're dancing a bit." A flutter rippled under her hand. "Would you like to feel?"

It was hazardous having him touch her so soon after their kiss. But what could be more innocent than a father experiencing his babies' kick?

He reached out hesitantly and she took his hand. Pressing his palm against her belly where she'd most recently felt movement, she watched for his reaction.

His warm hand tensed as if he was about to pull away. "I don't feel anything."

She held him in place. "Wait."

He did, but with tension radiating from him. A quick glance at his eyes, the fire sparking in their dark depths, told Ashley that his touching her would never be completely innocent. An answering heat curled inside her.

Then his eyes widened, his mouth opening in surprise. His hand cupped more firmly against her, and he was rewarded with an even stronger motion.

"I felt it." Awe colored his voice. "Was that a foot?"

Ashley laughed. "More likely a bottom. Feet are pretty small at six months."

He brought his free hand up to the other side of her belly. "Do they do this all the time?"

"No, fortunately. Although Sara's been warning me they'll be doing the can-can by the time the eighth and ninth month roll around. With two of them in there, I'm anticipating a lot of sleepless nights."

"My mother—" He yanked his hands away as if burned. The grief she'd seen earlier in his face returned like a whirlwind. "I have to get back to work." He strode toward the door.

Puzzling over what had just happened, Ashley tried to push away the empathy that rose up inside her. It was a losing battle. She hurried out the door.

He was nearly to the bottom of the stairs when she called to him. "Jason."

He didn't turn, but he stopped, hand gripping the rail. "What?"

His sharp tone nearly changed her mind, but she plowed ahead. "I'm going to make dinner after my nap. Will you join me?"

His long fingers looked ready to wrench the ornately carved wood from its moorings. He answered so softly, she could barely hear it. "Yes." Then he hurried across the living room toward the kitchen.

He exhausted her nearly as much as the two sprites growing inside her. Just when she thought she understood him even an iota, he changed directions, confusing her even more.

What had he been about to say about his mother? Back at school, he'd spoken of his father occasionally, once or twice mentioning his stepmother. He'd never said a word about his mother before now. Ashley didn't know if she was dead or alive.

Heading for the connecting door to her own bedroom, Ashley put the conundrum of Jason Kerrigan aside for the moment. She desperately needed some sleep. Since the pair tangoing inside her seemed to have taken a break from dancing, she would grab the opportunity for rest.

Setting her alarm so she'd wake in time to fix dinner, she sank onto the bed. Her head had barely hit the pillow before she fell asleep.

With the distractions Ashley had created, Jason nearly forgot about the scheduled teleconference. The meeting that had been pushed back from morning until afternoon had slipped again to four o'clock. So rattled by everything that had happened in the last hour or so, Jason sat down to read through e-mail and didn't check the clock again until three fifty-nine. He dialed into the conference line just in time.

Thank God he already had the notes written up. His mind felt scattered in a thousand different directions, his thoughts running in hyperactive loops. His brain's frantic circling had been a huge problem in elementary school, his cognitive processes moving so lightning fast, he could sometimes barely grab hold of one cogent concept. He'd learned to harness the rapid-fire workings of his mind in high school and college, but it still troubled him when he was under stress.

And life with Ashley was nothing if not stressful. The catastrophes, major and minor, of Kerrigan Technology he handled matter-of-factly, with the skill and know-how he'd amassed after years of interning with the corporation. The work he'd done toward his MBA had afforded him additional tools to solve the day-to-day issues he faced reviving his father's company.

But Ashley—nothing was simple with her. Every interaction with her either incited his libido or threw his mind into confusion. Her presence, the pregnancy, dredged up old memories he could have sworn were dead and deeply buried.

There wasn't anything from his childhood worth remembering. Not when it was all so heavily weighted with pain and guilt. He'd learned long ago a constant focus on the here and now was the only way he'd survive the past.

The conference call had been a success—his vice presidents and directors quickly championed the ideas he brought to them. In the course of the meeting, they crafted excellent strategies for offering displaced employees either comparable positions within Kerrigan Technology or decent severance packages that included two months use of an outside job placement service.

They all assumed he alone had devised the policies he'd presented. It didn't sit right to let them make that assumption, not when at least half the ideas came from Ashley. But how would he explain who she was? She wasn't a colleague or friend. He couldn't call her a girlfriend or lover.

Thanks for the kudos, but that plan to combine severance with career planning wasn't mine. That originated from the woman carrying my babies. Good God, he could just imagine the looks on his VPs' and directors' faces hearing that. Let alone what Maureen would say when it filtered down to her. He didn't know who, but his stepmother had someone within the company feeding her information.

It was 6:25 p.m. Ashley had left a voice mail telling him dinner would be at six-thirty. He'd heard his cell ring during the conference call and had barely resisted the temptation to put his managers on hold to take it. Even after the ringing stopped, his fingers itched to pick up the phone.

Another call from Maureen came through, as well, during the meeting, no doubt a continuation of his stepmother's harangue about Ashley. After her poisonous earlier call, Jason wasn't about to pick up the phone again to talk to her. What good would it do? No matter how many assurances he gave Maureen that Ashley and the babies wouldn't affect his stepmother's financial security, Maureen refused to hear.

Six twenty-nine. Closing the lid on his laptop, he pushed out of his chair and stepped into the early-evening sunshine. As he crossed the lawn, he caught glimpses through the dining-room windows of Ashley moving in the kitchen. The knots in the back of his neck eased just seeing her, even as his body responded in sensual anticipation. He didn't know what alarmed him more—the instant sexual spike or the baffling spark of joy.

Hand on the back door, he dampened both the physical and emotional reactions. He hadn't spent twenty years of his life shackling his mind's impulsivities to lose his grip over a woman. That one anomalous night wouldn't overturn the self-control it had taken years to master.

Pushing open the service porch door, he was about to enter when a flash of color caught his eye. Beside the door, in a bed nearly overgrown with weeds, three brilliant coral flowers waved in the early evening breeze. One had already started to fade and no doubt all three would drop their flaming petals in another day or two.

He didn't even realize what he was doing until he'd done it—broke the three stems one by one to gather the tall stalks in his hand. Then he crossed the back door threshold with the flowers all but mocking him with their broad coral faces.

He might try to convince himself he didn't understand the impulse that had driven him to snip these last bits of summer from their bed. But when he stepped into the kitchen and Ashley turned to face him, he knew exactly why he'd done it. Because his reward was instantaneous the moment she saw the flowers.

Ashley smiled.

Chapter Seven

The first month of the school year flew by, the days a mix of excitement, hard work and occasionally sheer panic. What she'd learned at UC Berkeley's School of Education didn't always translate into a real classroom filled with complex and sometimes problematical children. Not even her student teaching prepared her fully for the quirkiness of her own classroom, operating without the safety net of a master teacher.

But where the challenges in the classroom were exhilarating, the daily confrontations with Jason were exhausting. Their first shared dinner went well enough, starting with the shock of his gift of flowers. He'd seemed as surprised as she was as he'd given them to her, almost as if he wasn't sure how they got into his hand. Their conversation that night had been reasonably congenial and she'd almost been able to relax.

The standing invitation to dinner she'd offered had made sense at the time. They both had to eat, and his cottage didn't have a kitchen. She couldn't expect him to go into town every night and it was easier to cook for two than for one.

It should have been simple enough to deal with Jason in such small doses. Only an hour each night while they ate, then cleaned up after. They could get to know each other to some degree and begin the discussion she dreaded but would just as soon get through—what would happen after the babies were born.

But if they talked about anything, it was what had happened in the classroom that day or the current status of the recent Kerrigan Technology acquisitions. Whenever she tried to bring the conversation around to the subject of the babies, he found a way to sidestep her attempts.

He disappeared every weekend, leaving either late Friday or early Saturday, not returning until nine or ten on Sunday. She assumed he went home, but he didn't share that part of his life at all. She knew everything about his work at Kerrigan Technology, the projects he'd assigned his staff, the status of the construction of a cutting-edge tech lab in New Mexico. Nothing about his personal life.

So when Ashley sat down at her laptop computer on a Sunday afternoon four weeks after she'd moved into the Victorian, she tried to tell herself she was justified in doing a little research on Jason Kerrigan. Jason had set up a cable modem for her in the spare room on the other side of the nursery. For the first time, she was able to access the Internet at home rather than use the wireless hot spot at the Marbleville County Library.

She couldn't shake the sense of guilt she felt as she typed Jason's name into various search engines. Didn't she need to know more about him? He was the father of her babies; she ought to have at least a minimal amount of background on him. If he wouldn't open up to her, she'd have to ferret out the information herself.

At first her searches turned up nothing new, only a plethora of hits concerning Kerrigan Technology. She quickly scanned the list, then went to the company's Web site. The link to the CEO led her to a short and sweet biography of Jason, accompanied by a head shot.

Did he never smile? His expression was as cool and distant in that digital image as the face he showed her every night at the dinner table. That unchanging facade was as unmoving as stone. Even when they'd touched, kissed, only the fire in his eyes betrayed what his impassive face would not.

The sound of a car door slamming startled her out of her contemplation of Jason's image. As quiet as it was, the Mercedes had glided past the house to the guest cottage without her noticing. For the first time in weeks, Jason was home early on a Sunday, and she felt as guilty as a child caught stealing cookies.

Jumping back to the search page, she reflexively typed in the first phrase that popped into her mind, one she'd obsessively searched nearly every time she logged on to the Internet. The list of hits from her father's name, Hank Rand, replaced her previous search for Jason. A quick glance told her they were the same handful she always found, none of them her own father.

She heard Jason's key in the back door, then the rattle as he opened it. He called for her as he moved through the house. "Ashley?"

She would have just as soon met him downstairs, but at seven months, she moved even slower than she had four weeks ago. "Up here!" she shouted in response, then braced her hand on the computer desk for leverage.

She'd barely gotten to her feet before he entered the room. "You're home early."

He slowed as he drew closer. His hand reached out as if he intended to touch her, then dropped to his side. "I had to get back." His gaze fixed on her.

He might as well have touched her, the way her skin tingled along her bare arms. The short-sleeved dress she wore suddenly seemed far too insubstantial. She burned to know whether she was the reason he had to return to Hart Valley, but didn't want to think about why her importance to him mattered so much.

Finally he tore his gaze away, redirecting it to the laptop. "What are you doing?"

"Working." She shut the lid. "I didn't plan anything for dinner. I thought you'd be home late."

"I'll take you out." His gaze dropped to her belly. Now a new hunger shone in his eyes, a yearning. The fingers of his hand flexed.

He hadn't asked to touch her belly in the month since he first felt the babies move, and had declined when she'd invited him to again experience that exuberant life inside her. She'd thought he'd satisfied his curiosity that one time and it no longer interested him. But she couldn't deny the longing in those turbulent brown eyes.

Stepping closer, she took his wrist, laid his palm

against her belly. "They've been pretty quiet the last hour but earlier they were break-dancing up a storm."

His fingers widened as if to maximize their ability to feel the babies' movements, but the twins seemed disinclined to show off for their father. She kept her hand on his. "They're probably asleep. I think they prefer to save their antics for when I'm trying to rest."

He moved his hand across her taut belly, the warmth of his palm seeping through the thin knit of her dress. "Sometimes twins take turns sleeping." There was clear authority in the statement.

"Is that right?" She smiled. "Now you're an expert on twins?"

He pulled his hand away. "That's what I've heard." Turning away, he started toward the door. "I have to shower. I'll be back at six. We'll go into Marbleville."

She stared at his back as he left the room. Rousing herself, she followed to the top of the stairs. "Six-thirty," she called down, although she really didn't need the extra half hour.

Already halfway to the kitchen, he waved a hand in acknowledgment. She wanted to race down the stairs after him, grab hold of those rigid shoulders and shake him. Shout at him, *Tell me what's going on in there!* But even if her cruise ship of a body had the agility to catch up with him, she really wasn't sure she truly wanted to know what made Jason Kerrigan tick.

All that mattered was what he intended to do about the babies. Whether they would have to work out a custody arrangement or if he would be content with the occasional visit. And darn it, she was going to pin him down tonight. No more sidetracking.

After an hour writing up the week's curriculum, she decided she'd better catch a nap. She'd need to be well rested to bring Jason around to discussing the babies. If he wouldn't tell her anything about himself, his family, his life, so be it. She wouldn't force that issue. But they would map out their children's futures tonight.

Crawling onto her bed, she tugged the comforter over her and willed herself to relax. But darned if the twins didn't start their jig the moment she shut her eyes.

As Jason parked his Mercedes on the street, Ashley saw the Second Avenue Bistro in Marbleville still had their café tables out on the patio despite fall's arrival. At one of the tables, a young couple sat close together, gazes locked, the setting sun painting their faces pink and coral. Ashley couldn't help herself; their intimacy captivated her. What would it be like to be loved like that?

Jason opened her door and offered his hand. With his fingers woven in hers and his other hand on her arm to steady her, he eased Ashley from the car. He held on even after she was on her feet, his eyes on her face. The last of the Indian summer warmth on her skin, coupled with the romantic pair on the patio gave a weight and meaning to his intense gaze she knew was only fantasy.

He followed the direction of her gaze. "We can sit outside."

If they did, maybe she could pretend she and Jason were as enamored with each other as the young couple. She shook her head. "The sun's about to set. It'll be too cold."

He released her and they entered the bistro. She'd heard about this place with its fusion of country French and California cuisine, but hadn't tried it yet. The interior was light and airy, ferns hanging from the ceiling, the aroma from the kitchen tantalizing.

The hostess sat them back in a corner where the last of the sunset's deep orange light filtered through the blinds. With the menu to hide behind, Ashley was tempted to put off the looming discussion again. Instead she set the menu aside.

"We have to talk, Jason."

He stayed buried in the menu. "We'll order first."

She plucked the plastic-coated cardboard from his hands. "Now."

Leaning back, he seemed to draw his barriers around him. "What?"

She didn't let his brusque tone deter her and laid the contentious issue out baldly. "What are we doing after the babies are born?"

"We take care of them."

"There is no *we*. You and I won't be together afterward, so I have to know what you intend to do."

"I intend to support my children." His thumb tapped on the table, a study in agitation.

"You mean financially."

"Of course."

"*Just* financially," she clarified.

Closing his fingers around his thumb, he stopped its frantic movement. "How else?"

Relief and disappointment battled it out inside her. "Is that the extent you want to be in their lives?"

"I don't know anything about babies."

She felt a kick and her hand settled on her belly. "I don't know much myself."

"You're a woman." His gaze dropped to where she cradled her belly, and his fingers stretched toward her, although his hand stayed put. "Women have instincts."

"You think you don't?"

"About business. About technology. Numbers and calculations." Gripping his water glass, he took a drink. "What do I know about a child?"

As his thumb started its fidgety bounce again, Ashley grabbed his hand. "You could learn, just like I will."

Why was she trying to persuade him? Wasn't his absentee fatherhood exactly what she wanted? If he wanted to be involved in the day-to-day raising of the twins, they'd have to have some kind of shared custody agreement. The babies would be away from her days or even weeks at a time. She wouldn't be able to bear it.

But he was their father. Hank Rand might have been the world's worst example of a dad, but that didn't change the longing she'd carried around for years for a good man to take his place. She'd seen her friends' fathers, knew what it was like to have a dad who smiled, who didn't drink, whose love for their daughters shone in their eyes.

Her own babies deserved that kind of love. If it wouldn't come from Jason, she'd have to pray she'd find another man who would take his place. Yet that thought just made her heart ache.

He tugged his hand away. "The babies will stay with you. I'll provide for all their monetary needs." When she took a breath to speak, he pressed his fingers against her mouth. "Don't tell me you don't want my money."

She only needed to tip her head back to break the connection. But his long fingers felt warm against her lips and she wanted to kiss them, just to see his reaction. Lifting her gaze to his, she saw the heat that never seemed to be quenched in his eyes. As big as she was at seven months, she still couldn't understand her pre-occupation with sex. But when she was around Jason, she couldn't seem to think of anything else.

His hand moved, cupping her cheek, his thumb brushing her mouth. The clatter of dishes, the ringing of the bistro's phone receded as he leaned closer. They weren't going to kiss each other anymore; surely they'd agreed to that. They weren't lovers. Why would they indulge in such intimacies?

He shifted to the edge of his chair, closing the distance between them. She eased nearer as his mouth covered hers, sighed as his tongue dipped inside. One brief foray, then he retreated, another slip inside and retreat. She felt ready to melt in her chair.

Her mind wandered in dangerous directions. What would it hurt if they made love? It would be awkward because of the babies, but women did that sort of thing all the time. Sara had said she and Keith had been as passionate during her pregnancy as they had before.

Jason's fingers dived into her hair as he tightened his hold on her. His mouth felt so hot as it moved against hers, it stole her breath. She dug her fingers into the front of his knit shirt, the flexing of his muscles an aphrodisiac. She wanted nothing more than to be back at the house, with him in her bed, to take their kiss further, deeper.

She dimly heard footsteps, someone clearing their throat. Then finally an impatient "Excuse me?"

Ashley jolted back, banging her elbow on the corner of the table. Her cheeks hot with embarrassment, she flicked a quick glance up at the waiter standing there before she fumbled for the menus. Hand shaking, she passed one over to Jason.

The waiter tapped his pen against his order pad. "No question where those came from," he said with a pointed look down at Ashley's belly. "And I'm guessing you've been married less than a year."

She wasn't about to discuss her marital status with the waiter. Choosing something at random from the menu, she gulped down half a glass of water as the waiter left the table. The babies seemed to have picked up on her edginess, executing an energetic water ballet inside her. She pressed her hands there, wishing she could quiet them, to give herself a moment's peace.

Jason's thumb had started rapping on the table again. "What's the matter?"

"What do you think? You kiss me, make me completely crazy…"

His jaw worked. "I'm sorry."

"Hey, I was along for that ride." She could still feel the sharp awareness beating inside her. "No need for an apology."

"I would have thought…" He looked away, and she was shocked to see color rise in his cheeks. "You're pregnant. I would have thought…"

"Me, too. For God's sake, I'm as big as a house. But…" She dragged in a breath. "It must be hormones." *Because I want you so badly, I could scream.*

The waiter, smirking, dropped a basket of warm bread on the table. Ravenous and grateful for the distraction, Ashley grabbed two thick slices and the crock of butter from the basket. She wolfed down both pieces of tart sourdough without a jot of shame for her greed.

When her meal arrived, she was glad she'd eaten the bread. As distracted as she'd been, she'd ordered one of those froufrou salads filled with greens she didn't recognize, topped with an oily dressing that didn't sit right with the first mouthful. Picking the chicken out, she filled up on the meat and sourdough.

Buttering the last slice of bread, she leaned back with a sigh. "I'll set up the childbirth prep class with Sara, then."

He dropped the French fry he was about to eat. "What?"

"I'm assuming you won't want to coach me."

Emotions rampaged across his face—a purely male panic, uneasiness, sharp interest. "Why not?"

"You'd have to be in the labor room with me, then the delivery room when the babies are born. I just thought if you don't intend to be a father to the twins—"

He narrowed his gaze. "I'm their father."

"But you won't be involved in their life later. Does it matter if you're there when they're born?"

She saw the pain for only an instant before the walls closed in. "It's my responsibility. To you. To the babies."

"You have a right to be there," she said, although the thought of having him with her, when she would be at her most vulnerable, unsettled her.

He tugged his PDA from its holder on his belt. "When are the classes?"

"They start this week. Saturday mornings."

"Saturday." He fiddled with the stylus of his PDA.

"Ten to noon. I know you usually go back home for the weekends."

"Yeah."

"I thought you were getting your work done here, remotely."

"I do." He tapped away with the stylus. "How many weeks?"

"Four." She shouldn't even ask the question, but she was burning to know. "Then what do you do on the weekends?"

He slipped the stylus into its slot and the PDA into its holder. "Take care of personal business."

Curiosity still nipped at her, then her mind took a startling leap. "Are you dating someone? Is there someone in San José that you—"

"Good God, no!"

"I'd understand." Her stomach clenched as she spoke the lie. "You didn't hear from me for six months. You could have met someone—"

His hand dropped over hers. "There's no one. I haven't dated since you...since we..." His jaw flexed. "I've been too damn busy to think about anything but work and my father's affairs."

She'd forgotten about his father, that he must have been grieving for much of these last several months. That explained the sadness she sometimes saw in his eyes. "I didn't realize you were so close."

"I barely knew the man." There was no mistaking the bitterness in his tone.

"But you loved him."

He rubbed at his brow, as if to relieve the tension. "I wanted to."

Her heart ached at that stark declaration. Jason turned his attention to paying the check, signing the credit card receipt. The mask of indifference still guarded his face, but she felt as if she'd seen inside a window he didn't even know had been opened.

As they drove back home, Ashley wished there was something she could do to heal that deep inner pain. She had her sister to talk to when the ghosts of the past intruded. Jason seemed to have no one.

"If I can help you with anything—"

"I don't need your help." His harshness should have forestalled her, but she had to try again.

"If you ever want to talk." She put a hand on his arm to stop his immediate refusal. "About anything. You can talk to me."

He kept his eyes on the night-shrouded interstate. By the time they'd reached the house, Ashley had given up any hope that he would answer her.

He parked in the rear by the guest cottage and walked her to the back door. He unlocked it for her and opened it.

She stepped inside. "See you for dinner tomorrow night."

He moved away, starting toward his cottage. Halfway across the lawn, he stopped and turned toward her.

"Thank you." Two simple words, then he strode off into the darkness.

Chapter Eight

Jason had made it without a hitch through the first class at Marbleville County Hospital. He'd downloaded articles from the Internet, read up on childbirth preparation, had an idea what to expect. There wasn't much touching during that first session, so it hadn't added fuel to the fire that never seemed to quench when he was around Ashley.

But now, class number two, she lay back against him in his arms. She puffed through the breathing as he stroked her belly as instructed, her skin warm under the silky maternity top she wore. Far bigger than any of the other four women, all bearing singles, she outmatched them in beauty and sensuality.

She huffed through another set of breathing exercises. The rise and fall of her breasts was riveting. He shouldn't be staring, should be listening to the teacher's instruction. But years of forcing his brain to comprehend the verbal cues most people registered and processed without effort didn't prepare him for Ashley, her body soft and warm, her fragrance overwhelming. The instructor's words rolled over him, incomprehensible.

She shifted, wriggling even more snugly against him. His body already at full alert, he felt himself grow harder. Thank God there was a pillow between them or his lack of self-control would become crystal clear to Ashley.

Surreptitiously he checked his watch. Three minutes until noon. Just a few more minutes of sensual torture, then they'd drive back to Hart Valley for a quick lunch. He'd drop Ashley off at home, then drive to San José to spend the remainder of the weekend with his brother.

Mercifully the instructor called an end to the breathing exercise, and he helped Ashley up onto her feet. He held the pillow in front of him, not trusting the looseness of his pleated slacks to keep his secret. The other five couples held hands or stood with arms draped around shoulders or waists. The young pair that looked barely out of their teens locked briefly in a passionate kiss.

He looked away, not so much embarrassed, but not wanting his overheated imagination to get any ideas. He'd had trouble thinking of anything but kissing Ashley since their dinner at the bistro two weeks ago.

"Does everyone have a focus object?" the instructor called out above the noise of conversation. "We'll be using that next week."

As one, the women dove into their purses to produce the miscellaneous odds and ends they'd use during labor. Ashley had shown him hers before class—a palm-size teddy bear, its fur rumpled and barren in spots, one eye gone. Apparently Sara had given it to her years ago, not long after their mother had died.

She stared down at it now, her expression somber. No doubt she wished her mother was there instead of him. Likely she would have preferred her sister's presence to his. He still didn't understand why he'd pushed the issue, why he didn't just let the formidable Sara take his place.

He just couldn't stand the thought of anyone besides him and Ashley being the first ones to see the babies. Ashley had shown him the fuzzy ultrasound images, the twins barely recognizable. When they drew their first breaths, he wanted to see them, hear them.

She tucked the teddy bear back in her purse. "Were you heading home today?" Ashley asked as they followed the other couples out of the hospital meeting room.

"Yes." Three hours driving to San José, then three hours back tomorrow night. He had to see Steven, yet the wasted time weighed heavily on him.

The brilliant early-October sunshine glared on the pavement as they walked to the car. Ashley shaded her eyes as she turned to him. "Should we go to Nina's?"

"If you want." He unlocked the car, supporting her as she eased inside, then climbed into his own seat.

"We could just get sandwiches to take home." She tugged her seat belt in place, carefully tucking the lap belt under her belly. "You could get on the road quicker. Unless…"

"What?"

"Never mind." She fussed with her blouse, reminding him of how that taut skin felt.

"Tell me." He said it more harshly than he'd intended, his preoccupation with touching Ashley making him careless.

"There's an autumn festival tonight," she said as they pulled out of the hospital parking lot. "In the school cafeteria. A fund-raiser for the Hart Valley Community Center."

He'd seen the signs for it up around town. "I'll make a donation. Just let me know who to write the check to."

"That would be great." She lapsed into silence until they pulled onto Interstate 80. "But I wondered if you wanted to go with me."

He shouldn't. He had his responsibilities—to see Steven, to sign the last stack of papers regarding his father's estate. Still, he could visit with his brother on the phone, could have the papers sent by courier.

But a town festival…people packed in a small place, the noise deafening, a thousand sensory inputs competing for his attention. He usually avoided crowds, knew his limitations when it came to coping with too much clamor. But with Ashley there…

He glanced over at her and her smile undid him. "Let me make a few calls."

"Great." The light in her eyes washed away his doubts. "We'll do sandwiches, then. So you have more time."

She reached across the car, her fingers brushing against his arm. When she drew back, he captured her hand, folding it in his for just a moment. Unfamiliar emotions stirred inside him. Happiness. Contentment.

For once he thought maybe he deserved them.

* * *

An hour later he sat at his desk, his sandwich resting uneasily in his stomach. His conversation with Steven hadn't gone well, his brother anxious and agitated by yet another change in his world. Jason's promise to visit next weekend didn't satisfy Steven, who promptly hung up. When Jason called back, his brother's caretaker, Harold, assured Jason he'd smooth things over with Steven, but that didn't ease the guilt.

He dreaded the next call even more—to his stepmother, Maureen. She had the paperwork that needed his signature. He had to arrange for her to send them to him.

He was a grown man, but his stepmother still tied him in knots. She wasn't a cruel woman, but not especially kind, either. She'd had no patience for a little boy who couldn't sit still, who had to be sent home from his exclusive private school for misbehaving. When she married his father eighteen months after his mother's death, he hadn't yet learned the trick of burying the pain behind mental barriers. He'd act out, never quite understanding why he'd throw papers across the classroom or shout out the answers before the teacher called on him.

He mentally crossed his fingers, hoping she wouldn't answer and he could leave the message on voice mail. No such luck. She picked up on the second ring. When he told her why he'd called, that he wasn't coming home, he could hear the rancor in her silence.

"That woman's playing you," she said finally.

Jason tried to rub away the tension between his eyes. "I don't intend to have this conversation again, Maureen."

"Have you arranged for a paternity test?"

He gritted his teeth. "That is none of your business."

"It will be when she moves in here and turns me out." She managed to sound pitiful, outrageous for a woman who could chew nails and wash them down with tea.

"She doesn't want to move there. In any case, you have a life estate, Maureen. She couldn't turn you out."

"A life estate won't do me any good once she gets control of your money."

The urge to throw the phone across the room bubbled up. After nearly twenty years, his stepmother knew every button.

"Send the papers via the company courier. I'll bring them with me when I come down next weekend."

He hung up without waiting for her confirmation. Some motion outside the window caught his eye as Ashley exited the house. He thought she might be coming to talk to him, and that seed of happiness inside him blossomed again. Instead she headed straight toward the rear of the yard and out of sight.

Pushing back his chair, he got to his feet and left the cottage. He needed time with Ashley to clear his head, to wash away the unpleasantness of his conversation with Maureen.

A weight seemed to lift from his shoulders as he walked toward Ashley. She stood at the back fence, a blanket and a plastic trash bag in her hands, pondering a weed-filled flower bed.

She smiled as he approached. "This seemed like such a good idea a few minutes ago."

"What's that?"

"I saw the flower bed through the bedroom window and thought I'd come out and do some weeding."

He couldn't help himself; his gaze dropped to her enormous belly. "You can't be serious."

She laughed and the sound tugged at him. "I guess it made more sense in theory than in practical application."

"Give me the blanket." He spread it on the grass beside the flower bed, then took her hand. Supporting her back, he eased her onto the blanket. When she turned to try to reach the weeds, he stopped her. "I'll do it."

"I'll bet you've never pulled a weed in your life." Her eyes were bright with humor as she spoke.

"You'd lose," he said as he knelt on the blanket beside her.

She resituated herself so she faced him, her long legs in snug lavender leggings stretched out beside him. "Your father must have hired a gardener to maintain your yard."

"It's a three-acre estate. Not exactly a yard." He wrapped his hand around a mass of dandelion gone to seed. "But, yes. We have a gardener."

She opened the black plastic bag so he could toss the dandelion inside. "So you helped the gardener with the weeding?" She sounded dubious.

"I did." He yanked a hunk of crab grass from beneath a rosebush. "When I was a kid."

She held out the bag. "Was that your parents' idea?"

"God, no." He nearly laughed, remembering how scandalized Maureen was with her stepson grubbing around in the garden with the hired help. "I liked it. Being outside. It was quiet. I enjoyed the hard work."

"What were you like as a kid?"

His fingers tangled in the brilliant violet flowers of a patch of vetch, he hesitated before pulling the delicate plant free. "I was…difficult." Shaking the dirt loose, he dropped it in the plastic bag.

She caught his hand before he pulled it free, picking a scrap of violet from his arm. Her light touch sizzled through him, made him think of kissing her again. Before he could act on the notion, he turned his attention back to the flower bed.

"What do you mean, difficult?"

His stomach roiled. "I couldn't sit in a classroom or for more than five minutes at the dinner table. I'd run when all the other kids were walking, shout when everyone else was quiet."

"You were active."

"More than active. I was out of control." He shoved his hand between the branches of a rosebush, angling for another thick growth of dandelion. A thorn snagged the back of his arm, leaving a long red scratch. "Damn."

When he twisted his arm around to assess the damage, Ashley took his hand. "Let me see."

The scratch throbbed, but he barely felt it with Ashley touching him. "There are some antiseptic wipes in my bathroom upstairs. If you'll go get them, I'll clean you up."

He pulled his arm away. "Don't bother."

"If you don't go, I'll go get them myself. And me levering myself up off this blanket wouldn't be a pretty sight."

He had only to see the determination in her eyes to know she wasn't joking. He rose, brushing off his hands. "I'll go."

"Middle drawer left of the sink."

Leaving her in the afternoon sunshine, he went inside and upstairs. He didn't like the idea of invading the privacy of her bathroom, but he knew he didn't have any first-aid supplies of his own. He resolved to keep his mind on his task and not let his attention stray to anything remotely personal.

Fortunately, she kept the room neat, everything put away except her toothbrush and a water glass. After washing the dirt from his hands, he located the antiseptic wipes quickly and grabbed several. Resting in the palm of his hand, they reminded him of condom packets. That led his mind spinning in entirely the wrong direction.

He took a long breath to clear his head, but her cinnamon scent was everywhere. In the towel that hung over the shower rod, the bar of soap that sat by the sink, in the very air. He could so easily imagine her rubbing that soap over her wet body, drying herself with that towel, permeating everything she touched with her own fragrance.

Struggling to shut off the vivid images, he marched himself from the bathroom and back downstairs. He'd just managed to suppress the looping mental movie when he stepped outside and caught sight of Ashley. Leaning back on her arms, head tipped back, golden autumn sunshine spilling over her beautiful face, she took his breath away.

He wanted to drop on the blanket beside her and pull her into his arms. He wanted to hold her, to feel the life stirring inside her.

He slowed his steps as he approached, kept his hands to himself when he settled on the blanket. He dropped the foil packets of wipes beside her and turned his arm toward her. He wasn't sure how he would resist reacting to her touch.

Sitting up, she sighed, the soft sound erotic. Her fingers tearing open a wipe brought back a flash of memory—Ashley in his bed, ripping a different foil packet, rolling the condom over him. It was impossible to think of anything else but her fingers stroking the hard length of him.

The first brush of her hand on his arm was a shock. The warmth near his wrist where she held him still, the chill sting of the antiseptic. She daubed gently, cleaning half the long scratch, then opening another wipe for the rest. He was grateful for the nip of pain; it gave him something to think about besides pressing her back on the blanket and kissing her.

Once she'd finished, she threw away the trash and leaned back again. She'd slipped her shoes and socks off, and her bare toes were another erotic tease. The flower bed was only half-finished, but if he didn't walk away, he'd be doing something completely out of line.

Ashley gasped. "Oh, my." Her hand lay on her belly. "Somebody woke up."

He looked at her fingers spread out over her silky blouse and was shocked to see them jostled. Impulse had him reaching toward her, but he stopped himself and started to pull away again.

She took his wrist. "You've got to feel this."

When he'd touched her belly before, he'd felt a gentle rustling, as if one of the twins had sent a wave of cushioning fluid against the inside of her. There was no comparison between that subtle motion and the strong bumps against his hand he felt now.

It was an incredible sensation. Exhilaration burst inside him, an unfamiliar joy. It was like the giddiness he'd felt as a child running in the garden on a perfect summer day. Not on the Kerrigan estate's precisely manicured grounds, but in the unruly yard at the house in Mill Valley, north of San Francisco.

He cupped his other hand against her, as well, waiting for movement. What he felt grazing his palm was more a tickle than a bump, but it astounded him nonetheless.

He'd done this before. He'd blocked it from his mind, closed it off in that compartment where he kept his pain, the heartache too much to reexamine. But the memory had wriggled free of its box, showing him his mother's face, her body nearly as big as Ashley's, her smile as sweet as she urged her young son to feel the antics of his soon-to-be brother or sister.

He pulled his hands away and pushed to his feet. "I can't…" He couldn't stand to feel the joy anymore.

Ashley's brow furrowed as she gazed up at him. "Are you okay?"

"I'm fine." He reached down. "I'll help you up."

"Not yet. I want to enjoy the sunshine a little while longer."

He left her there with a promise to return in half an hour. Hopefully that would be enough time to shut away the pain and restore the numb neutrality inside him.

By the time they pulled into the Hart Valley Elementary School parking lot at seven, the sun had set and the warmth of the day had faded. As Jason helped her from the Mercedes, Ashley was glad she'd thrown a sweater over her short-sleeved dress. The pale-pink cardigan was too small to button over her ever-expanding belly, but it at least kept the early-October chill off her arms.

Jason stayed glued to her side as they stepped inside the noisy chaos of the cafeteria. He paid for their entry tickets, then stood frozen by the door as if working up courage to go inside.

She took his hand, locking her fingers in his. "Let's get something to drink."

Tension radiated off him as they cut through the crowd clustered around the buffet table set up near the door, then navigated their way around tightly packed masses of teenagers. He took the can of soda she handed him but didn't open it, his gaze roving over the milling throng.

Ashley took a sip of her strawberry soda. She gestured to the other side of the cavernous room where local crafters had set up tables. "It's a little less busy over there."

Holding her hand more tightly, he took in a long breath. "You need to eat."

"I can wait." Her stomach rumbled, exposing the lie.

"You can't." He led her to the end of the buffet line.

Nina O'Connell, serving up food with her husband Jameson, spotted her through the shifting bodies. Setting down her ladle, she made her way toward Ashley and Jason.

Nina took Ashley's arm. "Pregnant women should never have to wait for food." She started toward the front of the line.

Ashley kept her grip on Jason's hand as they threaded through the gathering. "I don't want to cut in front of everyone else."

Nina shouted above the clamor. "Any objection to letting the pregnant lady eat first?"

Voices called out in response. "No problem!" "Go right ahead!" "Leave some for the rest of us!"

Nina nudged her way in between J. C. Archer from Archer's Bakery, and Arlene Gibbons, who'd been about to pick up a paper plate to fill. With a smile for the wiry old woman, Nina said, "You don't mind, do you, Arlene?"

Arlene stepped back to give them room. "Not at all."

Nina plucked the sodas from Ashley's and Jason's hands. "I'll save a table for you."

Ashley would have inserted herself between Jason and Arlene, but he insisted she go first. She took a plate and spooned up some macaroni salad. Behind her, Jason followed suit.

As Arlene piled food on her plate, the old busybody speared Jason with her canny gaze. "So, you're the daddy."

His hand halfway to the bowl of fruit salad, Jason hesitated. "Yes."

"Took you long enough to take responsibility." Arlene reached past him to snag a roll. "Leaving that poor sweet girl on her own for six months." She clucked her tongue loudly.

Jason faced her dead-on. "How is that your business?"

Arlene's five-foot-even height seemed to expand by several inches. "You might all be cold-hearted in the city, but in this town neighbors look after neighbors."

"Ashley is none of your concern." His icy tone would have stopped a high-powered businessman in his tracks.

But Arlene was made of sterner stuff. She stepped in close to Jason. "She's my concern when you neglect your duties toward her."

"I'm taking care of her." He said it loudly enough for the now-rapt audience at either side of them in line to hear clearly.

"If you were taking proper care of her, Mr. Big Shot, you'd have done the right thing."

"I know what's right for her."

"Then make an honest woman of her, you nitwit." Arlene stretched up on her toes and got in Jason's face. "She's the mother of your babies. Marry the girl!"

Chapter Nine

Marry the girl!

Stunned by Arlene's crazy pronouncement, Ashley stared openmouthed at the old woman still peering balefully up at Jason. She could only imagine what she'd see in his face if he'd had it turned toward her— impatience, exasperation, irritation. She could barely grasp her own emotions, the muddle all the more alarming because of what it lacked; she felt no horror at the idea of marrying Jason.

Slowly turning his head, he looked back at her over his shoulder. She waited for his flat rejection of Arlene's lunatic notion. But he said nothing, just studied her, his brown gaze softening in a way she'd never seen before.

A strange little twinge throbbed in the vicinity of her heart. She couldn't let herself think about it.

Wedging herself between Jason and Arlene, she cast about for a way to defuse the old woman's bombshell. Remembering that Arlene and her husband just sold the Stop-and-Go market and gas station they'd owned for years, Ashley asked, "How are you and Mort enjoying retirement?"

The old woman shot another glare in Jason's direction. She was quick enough to recognize a diversion when she heard one. "We keep ourselves busy. Young man who bought the place calls Mort ten times a day."

As they continued through the line to the barbecue chicken and ribs, Ashley held her ground between the combatants. She could feel Jason's edginess, crackling like static electricity on a dry summer day.

Nina had staked out a table for them in a corner near the door, about as isolated and quiet a spot as could be found in the noisy room. After helping Ashley into her chair, Jason sat beside her, his gaze roving toward the exit as if seeking an escape route.

"Your food's getting cold," Ashley told him several minutes later when his plate still lay untouched.

He didn't seem to hear her, his focus still outside the boisterous room, as if the darkening night held all the answers for him. She wished she could find a few herself, the first being why the thought of marriage didn't terrify her the way it should.

It had to be lust. If they were married, there would be sex. If she wanted to, she could satisfy the urges that seemed to be constantly prickling under her skin. They could jump into bed every day of the week. Lust didn't care about emotions, about love. Despite feeling nothing but respect and a growing affection for Jason, her body would find a way around the awkwardness.

If it wasn't so completely wrong. Annoyed with the outrageous course of her thoughts, she returned her attention to her food.

Jason finally picked up his fork, although he still didn't eat. "She's right."

Ashley almost choked on a bite of roll. "Excuse me?"

His dark gaze fixed on her. "I should marry you."

"You shouldn't," Ashley said emphatically. "Arlene is nothing but an old busybody who can't resist poking her nose into everyone else's business. You can't give any credence to what she says."

"It's the best way to protect you and the babies."

"I don't need your protection." She set down the roll before she threw it at him. "I won't marry you, Jason. I don't love you."

She was only stating the truth. A man as impervious to emotion as Jason was shouldn't even flinch. He didn't, not really. But something flickered across his face before he looked away from her.

The impulse to apologize tugged at her, although she didn't know what she'd be apologizing for. The two of them marrying was about the most ridiculous idea she'd ever heard; he had to understand that.

But she didn't need to add to the walls he put around him. She had more compassion than that.

She touched his hand. "Jason—"

A crash and a cry of dismay cut her off. A dozen feet away from them a man and woman stood surrounded by a mess of spilled food and drink. A shame-faced boy hovered nearby, hands over his face. Zak Forrest, eight years old, Hart Valley Elementary's four-foot tornado. Ashley's most challenging student, Zak's biggest daily struggle was keeping himself in a chair and out of trouble.

Ashley would have expected Jason to be oblivious to the minor disaster. But as the affronted pair, newcomers to town that Ashley didn't recognize, berated Zak, Jason pushed to his feet.

She couldn't hear what he said to the boy as he bent to speak to him. There wasn't the least bit of anger in his body language toward Zak—although one hard look at the couple who had collided with the boy sent them on their way back to the food line. He simply talked things over with the eight-year-old, then the two of them retrieved one of the big trash cans that had been placed throughout the cafeteria. Zak's side dragged on the floor, but Jason neither scolded him for it nor took over carrying it himself.

They worked together to clean up the mess, gathering up plates, napkins and cups, mopping what they couldn't pick up with cleaning supplies Nina produced from the janitor's closet. Once they were done, Jason shook Zak's hand. The boy beamed as he craned his neck to look up at Jason.

Zak had vanished into the crowd by the time Jason returned to the table. She'd never seen him so relaxed, the tension that usually knotted his shoulders eased.

He picked at the cold chicken on his plate, tearing off a bite or two of his roll. "Twenty years ago," he said quietly, "that was me."

He was so tightly controlled, it was hard to imagine. But she supposed that was exactly why he disciplined himself so harshly—to keep the impulsive behavior in check.

She spotted Zak across the room, helping a toddler who had stumbled back on her feet. "He has such a good heart. Not a mean bone in his body. And he tries so hard."

Jason pushed his plate aside. "But he still gets in trouble."

"He needs more one-on-one than I can give him."

Jason watched the boy, now zigzagging toward the door. Zak flung himself outside, his yell fading as he ran across the playground.

Jason turned to her. "I could come in. Tutor him like I did the high-schoolers in Berkeley."

How could she handle having Jason in her domain? But how could she say no?

"That would be great." The twins seemed to pick up on her misgivings, starting a gentle tango inside her. "Tuesdays and Thursdays would be good. From ten to noon we have independent activities."

"Count on me, then." Jason's mouth curved in the briefest of smiles. "By the way, he doesn't believe there are only two babies in there. He thinks there must be at least ten."

She dropped her head in her hand in mock despair. "Am I that huge?"

He took her hand, folding her fingers in his. "You're beautiful," he said, then brought her hand to his mouth. His kiss was so tender it almost brought her to tears.

The golden light of mid-October spilled through the windows of Ashley's classroom, casting a warm glow over the students gathered on the rug around Jason. As he read *The True Story of the 3 Little Pigs!* to the children, Ashley worked at her desk, going over the arithmetic homework she'd sent home yesterday. Drawing a happy face on the last student's paper, she lifted her gaze to watch Jason.

This was his second week volunteering, and what had started as a way to help Zak had developed into a reading session for the entire class each day before lunch. Jason still came in for two hours on Tuesdays and Thursdays strictly for Zak's benefit, and the boy had blossomed under Jason's single-minded focus. But the other students had gravitated toward Jason, as well, providing Ashley a glimpse of him she never would have guessed he had hidden inside.

He was wonderful with children. As cold and rigid as he behaved with other adults, she assumed he would be the same with youngsters. Even with the high-schoolers they'd tutored, he'd been reserved and somewhat brusque, but with the seven- and eight-year-olds in her class he was warm and funny, sending them into giggles more often than not.

Jason sat in one of the tiny chairs, knees almost up to his chin as he leaned forward with the book in his hands. As he acted out the part of the indignant wolf in the story, the room rang with children's laughter. Zak wandered the room as he always did during story time, tidying the floor and straightening shelves, a task Jason had assigned him early on. Jason knew the boy could listen better with his body in motion, and now Ashley let Zak work on his feet whenever possible.

When he closed the book, his gaze strayed to her, something he did often while he visited. He didn't quite return her smile, but his face softened in a way that set off an ache inside her. Not quite as distant with her as he had been, it seemed as if some of his walls had crumbled. There was still more unknown than known about Jason, but day by day he'd worked himself into her heart.

The bell rang and the children scrambled for their cubbies where they stored lunches and lunch money. Two or three of Ashley's students gave Jason hugs before they lined up at the door. Zak danced around him, begging him to stay for the afternoon.

After they'd walked the children across the playground to the cafeteria, Jason accompanied Ashley to the teachers' lounge. As usual, he'd brought sandwiches when he'd arrived, stowing them in the fridge. They'd eat together, then he'd return to the guest cottage to work the rest of the afternoon.

A few other teachers had already gathered and were clustered at one end of the large conference table. They called out greetings as Ashley and Jason settled in their usual spot on a worn-out sofa in the corner of the room. Jason retrieved their sandwiches and sodas, snagging a handful of cookies from a tray someone had set out on the conference table.

Jason laid Ashley's sandwich, drink and cookies on a tray he'd bought for her the first week, setting it beside her on the sofa. She sighed as she picked up half her turkey sub. "I'll be glad when I have a lap again."

One corner of his mouth curved up as he spread a napkin on her round belly. "At least the crumbs don't have far to fall."

She gave him a poke. "Small comfort."

He bit into his sandwich, nodding as another teacher

entered and waved hello. "Emma's starting to speak up more during story time."

"I've noticed." Only a few bites into her sub, she broke an edge off a chocolate chip cookie.

Jason grabbed her hand before she could get it to her mouth. "Lunch before dessert." Again the corner of his mouth quirked up.

"I can barely eat a decent lunch before I'm full. I don't want to miss out on chocolate chip cookies because I'm too stuffed from half a sandwich."

His hand curved around her belly. "You still have seven weeks to go."

She pressed her hand over his. "If I go full-term. Twins often don't."

His warmth soaked through the thin fabric of her maternity dress. "I did." He took his hand back then, taking another mouthful of sandwich.

She tried to parse out what he'd just said. "You're a twin?"

He nodded, his concentration on his sandwich. As always, he seemed disinclined to share anything beyond the bare minimum.

He'd mentioned a brother when he'd first arrived in Hart Valley. She'd had the impression it had been a much younger sibling, not a twin. "Does he live in San José?"

Taking a last bite of his sandwich, he washed it down with a drink of cola. "Yeah."

"Does he work with you at Kerrigan Technology?"

Pushing up the sleeve of his dress shirt, he checked the time. "I've got a one-o'clock conference call."

She caught his hand. "Is coming here a problem? I know you're busy with work."

He pushed to his feet. "Everything is under control."

"I know you're under a lot of pressure."

"The acquisitions are complete." His plate and napkin dumped in a nearby trash can, he fidgeted with the soda can. "There's nothing to worry about." He paced away from her, then back again.

"If you need to go—"

"I'll walk you back to your classroom."

"Lunch isn't over for another twenty minutes. You'll be late for your meeting."

He stared at her blankly, and it struck her that he'd lied before. He didn't have a conference call. He'd only used it as an excuse to sidestep her questions about his brother.

Was Jason's twin a black sheep? Some kind of wild child that burned through the family money, an embarrassment to the Kerrigans? Even identical twins could have entirely different personalities. Just because Jason was staid and responsible didn't mean his brother was.

Curiosity burning inside her, she would have loved to press him for more information. But she doubted he'd reveal any more than he already had.

She sipped her soda and nibbled at her sandwich. "Go on home. Ronnie can tow me back to class." The middle-aged woman who taught third grade next door had just entered the lounge.

"I'll see you at dinner." He took one step away, then returned to lean over her. To her surprise, he kissed her cheek, lingering a moment before he straightened. Then he strode to the door, giving a curt nod to the principal as he passed her.

A cup of yogurt and an apple in her hands, Ronnie

plopped down beside Ashley on the sofa. Acerbic as always, Ronnie said, "Not exactly mister warmth and sunshine."

It was only the truth, but Ashley felt compelled to defend him. "He's a good man. You should see him with the kids."

"Actually, a few of your students have told mine about story time. My kids are pretty envious." Ronnie peered at her closely. "I know it's none of my business…"

"When has that mattered in Hart Valley?" Ashley said with a smile.

Ronnie laughed. "I'm just wondering…are you two… I mean, marriage is the usual next step here."

The *M* word didn't sit well on top of the half sandwich and cookie. "Have you been talking to Arlene?"

"It's obvious he cares for you."

"Jason?" She shook her head to deny the impossible. "Of course he doesn't."

Ronnie shrugged. "Not every marriage has to be a great love match."

"I have to get to class. Can you help me up?"

Once Ronnie helped her to her feet from the low sofa, Ashley stuffed the other half of her sub in the refrigerator and headed out into the October sunshine. A brilliant blue sky arched over her head, and a faint breeze swirled leaves on the asphalt playground. The gorgeous day should have lifted her spirits; instead it set off a sharp loneliness inside her.

She had five minutes until the end of lunch bell. She'd left her cell phone on her desk when she went to lunch, and longed to use the few remaining minutes of solitude to call Jason. Exactly what she'd say to him, she didn't know, but she thought she might feel better if she heard his voice.

She went as far as to pick up the phone as she sat behind her desk. The display showed a missed call—Sara. Her sister rarely phoned during school hours, and unease nibbled at Ashley.

The voice-mail message Sara had left only said, "Call me when you can," so Ashley quickly dialed.

Sara answered almost immediately, as if she'd been waiting by the phone. "Aren't you in class?"

"Two more minutes. What's the matter?"

"I might have bad news."

Alarm burst inside Ashley. "Is something wrong with Evan?"

"We're all fine," Sara assured her. "It's about our father."

Old, ugly images tried to crowd into Ashley's mind; she tried to slap them away. "What about him?"

"He might still be alive."

Ashley sat frozen, only half aware of the students lining up outside her classroom window. "How do you know?"

"I don't know, not for sure. But there was a newspaper photo I found last year."

"You didn't tell me." The kids had started rapping on the window, so Ashley rose to open the door.

"I wasn't positive it was him. But then an Internet search turned something up. A Hank Rand arrested in Las Vegas."

Ashley forced a smile as her students filed past her. "It might not be him."

"Of course. There was no photo. But I thought I'd better tell you."

As the classroom filled with restless children, the noise level rose. "I'll have to call you later."

She hung up, wishing even more fervently she could call Jason. She doubted she could bring herself to tell him about her father, let alone the secret that even now she was concealing from her own sister. She ached for his protection nonetheless.

But with a classroom full of active minds to teach, she had no time to speak to Jason. If she didn't get them busy soon, they'd be running amok, Zak Forrest as their ringleader. Already several of them were out of their seats, milling around the room or visiting with other students.

"Zak!" she called out as the eight-year-old started a jig over by the cubbies. "You and Abby get out the paints. Joshua and Andrew pass out paper."

Order restored, Ashley glanced at her notes for the art lesson, doing her best to banish her father from her mind.

From his vantage point between the infant sleepers and baby bathtubs in Everything for Baby, Jason watched Ashley wander the aisles of the baby store he'd brought her to after their final childbirth preparation class. The silky dress she wore flowed over her rounded body like a waterfall of lavender and soft blue, the V-neck front dipping low enough to reveal her generous breasts. During class this morning, he'd had a hard time keeping his gaze away from that mysterious hollow. With each puff as she'd practiced her breathing, his hands had itched to explore.

Everything for Baby, an establishment as upscale as anything tony Granite Bay had to offer, sat in a secluded shopping area centered on a courtyard fountain, far from the clamor of the local Sacramento area malls. When he'd discovered last night at dinner that Ashley intended to purchase the babies' cribs at the Marbleville Consignment Store, he'd put his foot down. He'd be buying the rest of what she needed for the twins, and he didn't intend to listen to any more argument from her. A quick call to his assistant pinpointed the best place for high-quality furniture and bedding for infants. If Daisy wondered why he needed the information, she'd worked for him long enough to know better than to ask.

By the front windows Ashley paused to admire a display of mobiles, reaching up to wind the mechanism of a model hung with butterflies. As the mobile turned, the tinkling music barely audible, the light slanting through the window illuminated her like some stained-glass Madonna. Religion had never been big in the Kerrigan household, at least not after his mother died, but seeing Ashley now, drinking in her beauty, he could almost believe.

Lifting her gaze, she sought him out, smiling when she spotted him. He should have smiled back at her, knew that was the right response. Maureen had lectured him often enough about it. *Don't you know how to smile?* she'd ask him, usually when he'd been asked to greet a roomful of total strangers, all with their eyes on him. He'd force his mouth to curve, but it never seemed to satisfy Maureen.

Ashley at least seemed satisfied, whatever she'd seen in his face. Her smile softened, and her gaze stayed on him, through the clutter of mobiles and the racks of baby clothes. There were only a handful of other women in the shop and one other man, all of them occupied with their own business. None of them saw what he saw in Ashley's eyes. Maybe if one of them had, they could have helped him understand it.

Then she looked away, moving on to a table piled high with baby blankets. Jason found he could barely catch his breath. His brain started its restless circling and, with an impulse that had become habit now, he returned his focus on Ashley. The circling slowed, ceased.

He needed to call Steven. Shopping with Ashley today meant a third weekend without driving home to see his brother. The weekend of the autumn festival, he thought he might go over on Sunday, but then Ashley had asked him to help her finish the weeding. The next weekend Ashley's brother-in-law, Keith Delacroix, had called to ask if he'd give a hand at the ranch putting up a new barn. He'd said yes without thinking through his answer, surprisingly enough. That he'd enjoyed the day working with Keith, Jameson O'Connell and Gabe Walker surprised him even more.

He knew Steven wasn't happy with his absence. Steven had made that clear during Jason's daily calls, with anger and with tears. The guilt at disappointing his brother sat like a stone on Jason's shoulders. He'd have to make it up to Steven, maybe try to get down there during the week. But he didn't like leaving Ashley this far along in her pregnancy.

As she examined a thick quilted blanket in the same colors as her dress, Ashley spoke with another expectant mother. Their murmurings carried across the room, although he couldn't make out what they were saying.

Once, the other woman glanced at Jason over her shoulder, and it shocked him to see a purely feminine admiration in her face. She said something more to Ashley, whose gaze seemed to touch him physically. His body reacted and again he found it difficult to breathe.

Busybody Arlene's declaration rang in his mind. *Marry the girl.* The words had revisited him often these past two weeks since the autumn festival. He hadn't brought it up to Ashley since that night, but the idea wouldn't let him go.

In terms of nuts-and-bolts logic, it made sense—it was a sure way of protecting Ashley and the twins, made their legal standing crystal clear. As his wife, she would have easier access to his financial resources.

Maureen would grouse, but he'd already discussed with his attorney the possibility of signing over to her the San José mansion, lock, stock and barrel. If he set up a Kerrigan Technology satellite facility in the Sacramento County town of Folsom, Jason could conceivably move there and be only forty-five minutes from Ashley and the twins instead of three hours. He was company CEO; if he wanted to run the business from Folsom instead of San José, he could do it.

But marriage wasn't just about logic, especially for a woman. Love tended to be important to them, or at least some kind of affection. And he'd learned long ago he just wasn't wired that way.

It was true that the more time he spent with Ashley, the more comfortable he felt with her. The stress he'd felt when they'd first moved to the house, triggered by his constant sensual awareness of her, had eased. Not that he'd lost interest in her sexually—her pregnancy-ripe body still intrigued him. But watching her interact with her students when he visited the classroom, the way she smiled at him across the dinner table soothed the frantic workings of his mind. She calmed him, something no one in his life had been able to do—except his mother, and she was long dead.

But comfortable was a long cry from love. While he'd strong-armed her into moving into the house with him, he doubted that same tactic would succeed in persuading her to marry him. It would be easier to simply have his attorneys draw up the legal equivalent.

As Ashley started toward him across the store, his phone rang. He tugged it from the belt holder and stabbed the answer button. "Kerrigan. Hold on," he barked into the phone, then turned his attention to Ashley. "The cribs are upstairs. They have an elevator."

"Take your call. Then we'll go up."

He brought the phone to his ear. "Yes?"

"This is Harold."

His brother's caretaker. Knots gripped his stomach. "What's wrong?"

"It's Steven," Harold said.

"Another tantrum?"

Harold sighed. "I'm afraid it's beyond that, Jason. He trashed his room. Accidentally broke a window. Maureen's fit to be tied."

He could just imagine. "Put him on the phone."

He heard a discussion in the background, Harold's soft, kind tone, Steven's petulant replies. Finally Harold said, "Here he is," then a clatter as the phone was handed over.

"Hey, bro," Jason said. "What's going on?"

"I miss you." He could hear the tears in Steven's voice. "Please, please, come home."

Chapter Ten

Jason shoved the phone back into its holder and tried to relax the tension in the pit of his stomach. His thoughts seemed to chase each other—Steven needed him...he couldn't leave Ashley...he had to see his brother...Ashley needed him...Steven...

Ashley's hand on his arm anchored him, slowing the spiraling thoughts. "What's wrong?"

He took her hand. "I have to go home."

"Then let's go."

"To San José," he clarified.

"Fine. Let's go."

"I have to take you back to Hart Valley first." The time he would lose driving her up the hill upped his stress. Confusion threatened.

"You don't. I'll go with you."

There were reasons he'd wanted to keep Ashley separate from his world in San José, but for the moment he couldn't grasp them. "You shouldn't drive that far."

She tugged his hand, pulling him toward the door. "There are probably a dozen hospitals along the way if the twins make a surprise appearance."

He checked his watch as he pulled out of the parking lot, then handed his phone to Ashley. "Dial preset number three. Harold should answer. Tell him we'll be there by four."

Ashley made the call, identifying herself to Harold and relaying the message. Jason had given Steven's caretaker the barest explanation of the situation with Ashley. Harold had no doubt borne the brunt of Maureen's displeasure over the unexpected pregnancy, but Jason knew the older man was such a gentleman, he would make his own judgment of Ashley when he met her.

Ashley set the phone on the Mercedes's center console. "He said he managed to convince Steven to take a nap."

Relief eased his too-tight grip on the wheel. "That's good."

He could feel her gaze on him. "I'm not about to demand you explain, but I'd like to know what's going on."

He glanced over at her, then back at the road. Few people knew about his brother's condition, no one beyond Maureen, Harold and the battery of doctors who had treated him over the years. With the rapid turnover of the high-tech industry, there was no one left on the staff of Kerrigan who remembered the accident twenty years ago. It wasn't something Jason discussed, and Maureen scarcely acknowledged Steven's existence, let alone confided with her friends about him.

Jason would have to tell Ashley something, at least the bare minimum. "Steven is my twin brother. He has…problems."

"Something he was born with?" Her fingers curved protectively around her belly. "Something that the twins—"

"Nothing like that." He merged onto the freeway and accelerated past a semi. "He was fine, perfect when he was born. It was an accident. When we were eight."

"Was he paralyzed?"

"Severe head trauma." The words still tasted bitter in his mouth. "He's brain damaged."

"Oh, Jason. I'm so sorry."

He didn't deserve her sympathy, didn't want her soft voice easing his pain. If not for him, the accident wouldn't have happened in the first place.

He doused the warmth her kindness had set off inside him. "He was brilliant, even as an eight-year-old. Smart, creative. Everyone liked him."

The good brother. Jason had taken the other role, of the troublemaker.

"And now?" she asked.

His throat constricted at her quiet tone. He took a breath, swallowed to get the words out. "He has the mental capacity of a six- or seven-year-old."

Her hand brushed his shoulder. "That must have been so tough for you, to have your brother hurt."

Again the softness spread inside. Imagining a fist closing around the emotion, he squelched it. "You can stay in the car when we get there."

"Why would I want to do that?"

He wasn't going to sugarcoat it. "Steven has mood swings, tantrums. There's no telling how he'll be today."

"Could he hurt me? Or the babies?"

"No! He would never touch you." Jason knew that with a bone-deep certainty. "He gets frustrated. It's as if he remembers…"

"How he was before?"

"Yes."

He felt her gaze on him. "If you don't mind, I'd like to meet your brother."

"As long as you know—"

"I know. It might not go well. But he'll be the twins' uncle. We should at least meet."

A thread of happiness unwound inside him. "I'll bring you in, then." With any luck, Maureen wouldn't even be home.

They drove on, past Sacramento and Davis, west toward the interchange south toward San José. Ashley sat quietly beside him, staring out the window. As they traversed the East Bay, a compulsion to reach out to her rose inside him, and he had to wrap his fingers even more securely around the wheel to keep from taking her hand.

Twenty miles north of San José, she said, "I understand now."

He spared her a quick glance as traffic slowed near the Interstate 880 interchange. "What?"

"Why you're so good with the kids in my class."

"I just read to them. It's no big deal."

"You connect with them. Zak especially. As if you know exactly how he feels inside."

He wasn't sure how he felt inside himself, let alone

comprehend the workings of an eight-year-old. "Most of the time, I'm guessing what to do next."

"You think I don't?" She laughed. "You'll connect with the babies, too, Jason."

He should deny the possibility, inform her she was completely wrong. But that stark honesty warred with a burning desire to believe he had at least the smallest capacity to love and care for his children.

It might be utter fantasy, but for the moment he chose to ignore the facts—that he was no more equipped to be a father than he was to defy gravity and fly.

The road to the Kerrigan mansion wound its way through a neighborhood of massive homes secluded behind high walls and thick hedges. If Ashley had needed further confirmation that she didn't belong in Jason's high-flying world, this was it. She couldn't imagine herself living in any of these palatial estates, let alone knowing anyone who lived there.

But how well did Jason fit in this rarified atmosphere? Surely he felt completely at home at Kerrigan Technology; he'd always seemed comfortable in the world of business. But considering his growing tension as they rolled up to a stout wrought-iron gate set within six-foot brick walls, she guessed this wasn't truly his universe, either.

Pressing a button on a remote clipped to his sun visor, he waited as the gate rolled aside before driving through. The driveway terminated in front of the house, circling around a stone fountain tossing water to the sky.

"Did you ever play in the fountain?"

"Once."

When he didn't elaborate, she prodded, "Only once?"

Stopping the Mercedes near the front door, he yanked on the parking brake. "Maureen made sure I didn't do it again."

The three-story Tudor fronted with stucco and stone loomed above them as they approached the arched entry. The broad expanse of green lawn should have been welcoming, but there was something about the austere lines of the house that made Ashley want to return to the safety of the car.

To her surprise, Jason rang the doorbell. "Don't you have a key?" Ashley asked.

"I do."

"I thought the house was yours."

"It is." He rang again. "For now."

"Then why not just go in?"

"Maureen prefers it this way."

Finally she heard footsteps. A man in formal dress with a dour face opened the door. "Mr. Kerrigan," the man said before his gaze narrowed on Ashley. The distaste in his expression was clear.

"Mrs. Kerrigan isn't home," the man told them. It was obvious from his tone that he thought they didn't belong there in Jason's stepmother's absence.

Jason took Ashley's arm. "We're just here to see Steven."

Reluctantly the scowling man opened the door wider and stood aside. Jason escorted her through an immense foyer, their footsteps clicking on the Italian tile and echoing off the twenty-foot ceiling. To their left, an archway flanked by white marble columns led to an overfurnished living room. Just ahead, twin staircases lined with wrought-iron balustrades topped by sleek oak banisters led to the second floor.

As they climbed the stairs, Ashley could feel the man's stare. She leaned close to Jason to whisper, "That isn't Harold, is it?"

"Good God, no. That's Renard. Maureen's butler."

At the landing Ashley took a quick look back at the disapproving Renard. "Then he's never been in charge of Steven?"

"Not Steven. Just me."

Ashley's heart fell as she pictured Jason under that iron hand. There couldn't have been much love between them. Renard still watched them, as if he suspected they'd steal the family silver at any moment.

As severe as the architecture had been outside, the interior decor made up for it lavishly. If a frill could be added to a crown molding or wall treatment or tabletop, it had been piled on. Ornaments littered every surface and heavy oil landscapes crowded the walls, their frames overpowering. This was a house where every-thing would be off-limits to a little boy. She imagined Jason had gotten his hand slapped more than once.

A door at the end of the hall stood slightly ajar. Jason tapped lightly. An older man with gentle eyes poked his head out. "He'll be so glad to see you." He smiled at Ashley. "You must be Miss Rand. I told Steven you were visiting, as well."

They stepped into the bright, sunny room with its well-worn sofa and chairs, bookcases full of children's books and DVDs, and a television on a sideboard. Behind a half-drawn drape, a bed sat in an alcove at the far end. Where everything else in the house had been elaborately decorated, this room was simple and cozy. Ashley guessed that whoever had embellished the rest of the mansion hadn't laid a finger on this space.

"I'm Harold." He folded Ashley's hand in his.

"Where's Steven?" Jason asked.

"After he helped me clean up, he wanted to shower and change. He'll be out in a minute."

Other than a board placed over one of the windows overlooking the backyard, there wasn't much evidence of Steven's tantrum. There were books scattered here and there and an old Rubik's Cube on an end table.

His hand at the small of her back, Jason tensed his fingers against her. "You should sit."

"I'm fine."

"You shouldn't be on your feet so long." He urged her toward a plump recliner.

She resisted. "I sat all the way here."

A door near the sleeping alcove opened and a young man stepped into the room. His hair was longer than Jason's neat, conservative cut and he wasn't quite as lean. But the face was nearly identical, the brown eyes the same, the mouth a duplicate. Then that mouth smiled and the similarity vanished. Because Jason never smiled.

His wide grin splitting his face, Steven hurried across the room, arms flung out. "You're here!" He embraced his brother so powerfully, Ashley could hear the air puff out of Jason's lungs. Jason hugged him back, the gesture so loving, so genuine, it tugged at Ashley's heart.

Steven turned to Ashley, his expression as welcoming as Renard's was not. "Is this your girlfriend, Jason?"

Jason took her hand. "This is Ashley."

Steven stared at her belly. "You're having a baby."

"Twins," she told him.

He grinned even wider. "Like me and Jason."

Steven threw his arms around her, although his hug was more careful than the one he'd given his brother. When he pulled back, he patted her rounded tummy. "Hi, little babies. When will they come out?"

"Another month or so," Ashley told him.

"Will you bring them to visit?" he asked, his expression eager.

"Of course," Ashley assured him. "As soon as possible."

He grabbed her hand and towed her over to the sofa. "Come read my favorite book."

They sat together on the sofa, Ashley reading *Owl Moon* aloud, Steven following along, his lips moving as he mouthed the words. Jason watched them, a torrent of emotions in his eyes. She longed to know what he'd locked up inside him, wished fervently she could do something to soothe him.

As she read, Steven ran his finger over a drawing of an owl with wings outspread. That he looked so much like Jason, that his manner was so sweet, made the tragedy of the accident that injured him all the more heartrending. Ashley still wondered what exactly had happened—had he fallen and hit his head? Could someone have hurt him? She felt sick at the thought of someone hurting an innocent child.

But as usual Jason had told her only so much and no more. Maybe it was none of her business. Or maybe their lives had become so entwined it was time he opened up to her more. She doubted she would easily convince him of that.

After *Owl Moon,* Steven pulled out a stack of Berenstain Bears books and begged her to read them, too. They struck a bargain—they'd take turns reading the pages. Steven stumbled over the words sometimes, but Ashley kept up a constant stream of praise.

At some point Jason's phone rang and he excused himself to take the call. Before he slipped out the door, his gaze found hers, and the gratitude in his eyes carried across the room.

When he'd first arrived in Hart Valley, she'd wondered if he had the ability to love anyone, most particularly the babies she carried. Seeing him with his brother, maybe the only one in his life he could trust utterly, a spark of hope lit inside her.

Yet if he could connect with his children, if he could show them the love he showed his brother, how could she justify sole custody? Wouldn't it be best for the twins, for him, if he had the chance to care for them? Could she let them go to their father, knowing how bitterly she would miss them? But how could she not? They deserved to know both their parents.

There was one solution, the crazy bit of insanity Arlene Gibbons had brought up at the autumn festival. If she and Jason were married, they would both have the benefit of living with the twins full-time. It would be the best of all possible worlds for the babies.

But it would likely mean she'd have to move from Hart Valley, a place that had become home to her, and quit the job she'd come to love. Could she do that, knowing it was best for their babies?

Could she live in this place with a man who was still largely a stranger to her? The empathy she felt for him, her compassion for a man whose childhood had been painful didn't translate into love. And wasn't love the most essential element of marriage?

"Ashley?" Beside her, Steven pushed *The Berenstain Bears and the Trouble with Friends* into her hands. "Can we read this now?"

"Sure." She opened the book and began to read the first page, her troubled thoughts weighing heavily.

She read with Steven until dinnertime, Jason returning to sit in one of the recliners, more relaxed than she'd ever seen him. Harold had gone down to deliver the bad news to Renard that they'd be staying for dinner, and Ashley had a clear mental image of the snooty butler turning up his nose in disgust. Apparently, Steven usually ate in his room with Harold, but tonight he'd eat downstairs with Ashley and Jason. So excited that he'd be sharing dinner with them, it took all of Harold's powers of persuasion to entice Steven to put away his books and wash up in the bathroom.

Once they'd left the room, Ashley took Jason's hand to rise from the plump sofa. "Is your stepmother here?"

Jason's grip tightened briefly on her hand. "She came home an hour ago."

"She didn't come up to say hello."

"She's—" Jason hesitated "—resting. She'll join us for dinner."

Filled with trepidation, Ashley held fast to Jason's hand as they descended the stairs. Steven's joyful attitude had shifted once he'd learned Maureen would be at dinner, as well. Ashley half expected some kind of Gorgon to greet them when they arrived at the formal dining room with its long, heavy table and stiff-backed chairs.

As diminutive as a young girl, her short blond hair impeccably coiffed, Maureen Kerrigan smiled as Ashley entered with Jason. The years had obviously been kind to her; she was likely in her fifties but looked at least a decade younger in her silk blouse and well-tailored designer slacks.

When her blue gaze flicked down to Ashley's belly, it seemed a normal enough reaction; everyone stared at her pregnant self these days. If her attention lingered there a bit longer, if her smile faded for an instant, Ashley supposed she could interpret that as parental disapproval of an out-of-wedlock pregnancy.

If not for the look in her eyes when she lifted them to meet Ashley's. Cold. Angry. Far more intense than censure.

She turned her harsh gaze on Jason. "I'd appreciate the simple courtesy of an introduction to your...friend."

Tension rippled off Jason. "Maureen, this is Ashley Rand. Ashley, my stepmother, Maureen."

Ashley pasted on a smile and put out her hand. "It's wonderful to meet you."

The woman hesitated before grasping Ashley's hand. "Jason never could learn even a modicum of politeness," she said, her smile not reaching her eyes. "I gave up long ago."

Ashley linked her fingers in Jason's. "He has always been a perfect gentleman with me."

Maureen again glanced down at the evidence of her

stepson's folly. "If only he exercised even a shred of self-control." She patted Jason's cheek.

A very unladylike urge welled up in Ashley to plant her toe in Maureen's well-dressed shin. Instead she let Jason seat her for dinner. He sat between Ashley and his stepmother's throne at the head of the table, Steven across from them. Edging his chair away from his stepmother, Steven kept casting worried looks Maureen's way.

Dinner seemed interminable. Renard brought out course after course, most of it fussily prepared and unappealing. As hungry as she was, Ashley couldn't stomach the goose-liver pâté and caviar, nor the wilted greens drizzled with oily raspberry vinaigrette. When Renard brought out a basket of rolls, the only plain food on the menu, Steven wolfed down three in quick succession. Ashley hoped she ate hers with a little more decorum.

The grandfather clock in the corner of the dining room seemed to scream out its ticks and tocks as plate after plate went back to the kitchen uneaten. If Maureen enjoyed the food, you couldn't tell from her dark looks as she ate. She glared at them in turn, her disapproval piling higher in the room until Ashley thought she'd drown in it.

The last course finally finished, Maureen dabbed daintily at her mouth with her napkin. "I would have ordered the cook to prepare dessert tonight, but Jason's a disaster with too much sugar. Aren't you, dear?"

Unlucky that Ashley's water glass was empty. She would have loved dumping its contents on the wicked-tongued woman.

Jason dropped his napkin on his plate and shoved his chair back. "We have to get back."

Steven looked crestfallen. "No, don't go yet."

"It's a long drive. Ashley needs her rest."

"Please." Tears threatened in Steven's eyes. "Stay a little while longer."

Jason smiled, the rare sight stunning to see. "Hey, bro, we'll be back again soon."

Steven rose so quickly, his chair fell backward. Tears spilled in earnest down his cheeks. "I don't want you to leave me with her."

Jason turned to Maureen. "What have you done to him?"

"Absolutely nothing," she insisted. "He's overly sensitive. You and Harold spoil him."

Leaning against the table, he bent closer to her. "What have you done?"

"Nothing!" Now she seemed flustered when faced with Jason's anger. "It's ridiculous. I make him sleep with the light off. There's no point wasting electricity all night. There's nothing to be afraid of in the dark."

Jason's hands fisted on the table and for a moment, Ashley thought he might strike his stepmother. He dragged in a breath, another, then another, then finally stepped away from the table and Maureen. Holding out his hand to Ashley, he helped her to her feet. "Let's go."

"Jason," Steven said, hugging himself.

"Don't worry, bro," Jason said gently. "I won't leave you here. Go upstairs and pack. You're coming with us."

Chapter Eleven

Steven bolted the moment Jason's words registered, racing from the dining room and upstairs. Another long look at his stepmother, then Jason turned to Ashley. "I'd better go up and help him."

Ashley squeezed Jason's hand. "Go ahead. I'll be fine here."

Ashley wrapped her arms around her middle as Jason left the room. Fixing her harsh blue gaze on Ashley, Maureen waited until the sound of Steven's door closing carried to them.

Her eyes narrowed on Ashley as she spat out her question. "How much?"

"I don't know what you're talking about."

"Of course you do. A cheap little tramp like you. How much to go away?"

Ashley shook her head, baffled. "Go away where?"

"From my stepson. From the area. Out of state if necessary."

Ashley tamped down her own surge of anger. "I'm not going anywhere."

Maureen snatched a bell from the table and rang it hard. "Don't think I don't know what you're doing."

Renard entered and, with a disdainful glance at Ashley, started clearing the table. Ashley pushed back to get well clear of him as he worked.

"I'm pregnant with your stepson's babies," Ashley said, trying to keep her voice even. "We didn't intend it to happen—"

"Oh, please. As if I believe that." She pushed to her feet and loomed over Ashley. "You planned this. You intended to trap my stepson one way or another. If he wouldn't marry you outright, you'd rope him in playing the pregnancy card."

The little Ashley had eaten roiled in her stomach. "Excuse me," she said, hands gripping the arms of her stiff-backed chair to lever herself to her feet.

As Ashley struggled up, Maureen looked as if she'd like nothing better than to shove Ashley back into the chair. Luckily, the woman kept that impulse to herself.

Now Ashley had the advantage, standing at least six or seven inches over the imperious Maureen. "I'll wait for Jason in the foyer."

Maureen grabbed her arm. "I can write a check right now. You don't even have to leave that Podunk little town of yours. Just tell Jason you want nothing more to do with him."

"Take your hand off me."

She dug her fingers in deeper. "You can't think you'll have any kind of life with him. He has no heart, not a shred of social skills. I did my best with him, but you couldn't beat a sense of responsibility into that boy."

Horror settled inside Ashley at this further evidence of the misery present in Jason's childhood. "He's a good man and he'll be a good father."

A vicious fire burned in Maureen's eyes. "What about when he loses control and he does something to hurt them?"

"He would never—"

The harridan stepped closer. "Who do you think caused the accident that hurt his brother?"

"He was eight years old!"

"You ask him. Ask him how he lost control. How he killed his own mother!"

The shouted words hung in the air as Maureen shifted her gaze from Ashley to someone behind her. Ashley knew before she turned to look that it was Jason standing there and that he'd heard Maureen's declaration. Guilt twisted Jason's face into a mask of pain.

He stepped into the room and took Ashley's hand. "Steven is ready. Harold will be coming, as well. He'll drive Steven in his own car."

With the exception of Hank Rand, Ashley had never hated anyone. What she felt for Maureen Kerrigan in that moment came close.

Steven and Harold were already in the foyer with luggage at their feet. Without a word the three men picked up the assortment of suitcases and headed for the door. Behind them, Maureen stood in the arched entrance to the dining room, unrepentant, her work done.

* * *

He would have to tell her. Maureen had exposed the ugliness he'd done his best to keep hidden away these past twenty years. Even if Ashley never asked, knowing she knew even a part of it meant he could never completely stuff it away again.

Night had closed in as they made their way through the winding streets back to the freeway. The expansive homes they passed sat shadowed behind high walls, no doubt hiding their own painful secrets. Whatever tragedies had taken place in those stately homes, Jason knew nothing about them; each moneyed fortress had kept to itself during his childhood.

It should have been a kid's fantasy land—wide green lawns to run and play on, enough money to buy any toy a boy could wish for. It might have been that if his mother hadn't died. Or if he could have been a different boy for his stepmother, a boy who could sit still, who could obey his parents instead of his impulses.

With a glance in the rearview mirror to be certain Harold was still behind them in his sedan, Jason pulled back onto Interstate 680 north. The two-and-a-half-hour drive would be more than ample to lay out the past for Ashley.

When she took a breath, Jason tensed, but she didn't ask the question he dreaded. "Had you thought about where Steven and Harold would stay?"

He had, and that solution had its own complications. "In the guest cottage. Steven can have the bedroom, and I'll set up a sleeping area for Harold in the living room."

"And what about you?"

He glanced over at her. Her fingers spread, she had her hands cupped on her belly. "I'll move to the house, to the spare bedroom." And be twenty feet down the hall from her.

She nodded. "I'll move my computer downstairs."

"I couldn't leave him there."

"No," Ashley said emphatically. "Absolutely not."

Jason wondered what other nastiness Maureen had shared with Ashley. His endless problems in school, the dozens of times Maureen got called into the principal's office because Jason Kerrigan simply couldn't behave himself in class. He doubted that when she married his father she'd expected to take on a troublemaker like him. Bad enough having a brain-damaged stepson; Steven at least could be cared for by hired help. But Jason's father refused to allow Maureen to employ a nanny for him.

Considering Maureen's treatment of him, Jason knew he'd have been better off with a nanny. Better the attentions of an aloof caregiver than his stepmother's calculated cruelty.

Even if he deserved it as penance for what he'd done.

Ashley turned to look behind her at Harold's white sedan. "We'll have to stock up on groceries. We'll be four for dinner instead of just two."

"Harold can take care of it." His impatience spilled over. "Good God, you can't ignore it, Ashley."

"Ignore what?" she asked, although from her tone, he suspected she knew.

"What Maureen said about Steven. About my mother." His palms ached from clutching the wheel.

She sighed, the soft sound a balm that would have

soothed him if not for that guilt he gripped so tightly. "What happened, Jason?"

What if when he told her everything, she pushed him from her life? It shouldn't matter…who was she to him, anyway? Just the mother of his babies, someone connected to him by an accident of fate. But to never see her again, to never see the babies…that hurt unbearably.

But he'd goaded her into asking, and he had to tell her. Even though twenty years after the fact, he still hated remembering the accident. He owed her a full telling of the story, even if it drove her away.

"We were on our way to Santa Cruz." The words came out rough-edged and he cleared his throat. "Kerrigan Technology was taking off like a rocket and UC Santa Cruz asked my father to speak at commencement. He'd gone ahead. We were meeting him there."

With crystal clarity, he could see himself in the back seat of the car, his brother beside him, his mother driving. They'd taken Highway 17 through the Santa Cruz Mountains, a treacherous twisting roadway nicknamed the bloody highway.

"Steven wasn't like me. He was quiet. A good kid. He could sit still in a car for hours coloring or flipping through a book."

Jason could barely keep his energy contained for ten minutes, let alone the forty-five it took to travel from San José to Santa Cruz. He could still recall the way the agitation built in him until he had to find an outlet.

"I started messing with Steven, making faces, pulling his hair, poking him. He did his best to ignore me. Then I took away his book."

Even at eight Steven had loved to read. Back then

Jason struggled to make sense of words on a page and he envied the ease with which Steven entered the world of story a book provided. But Jason couldn't seem to control the impulse that drove him that day.

"He tried to get the book back. I held it out of his reach. He's yelling, my mother's yelling. Still I wouldn't give it back."

Highway 17 wasn't a route that tolerated distraction while driving. His mother had never traveled that way before and she didn't have only squabbling eight-year-olds on her mind. She took her eyes off the road for an instant, but it was too much.

Sweat gathered under Jason's palms, and he held on to the wheel even tighter. The Mercedes jounced on the warning bumps and sudden terror burst inside him. He could go off the road in a heartbeat, cause an accident just as he had twenty years ago. Except this time it would be Ashley hurt, and the twins.

Flicking on his blinker to alert Harold, he took the next exit off the interstate and turned into the driveway of a roadside service station. He was dimly aware of Harold pulling up beside him, of Ashley waving Harold around them. The white sedan parked near the service station minimart and Harold took Steven inside.

Memories battered Jason, too horrifying to be grasped. He didn't want to talk anymore, wanted to lock them up again. But then he felt Ashley gently stroking his arm.

He dragged in a deep breath. "I caught a glimpse of a truck cutting in front of us from a side road. My mother swerved to avoid it. Impact. Then…"

Then no noise. His mother quiet as death. His

brother bloody. The car unrecognizable, mangled metal and plastic.

"Your mother…" Ashley said softly.

"Killed instantly."

"And Steven…"

"The car spun. Hit a tree on the driver's side. Where Steven was sitting. If I'd been on that side…"

Her hand stroked along his forearm, warm and soothing. "It wasn't your fault."

"I distracted her. If not for me—"

"The accident might still have happened."

"She would have seen the truck sooner."

"She might have. But it might not have mattered." She lifted her hand to his cheek, her touch eroding his defenses. "You have to let it go, Jason."

He shoved her hand away. "You don't know anything about it!"

His shout seemed to reverberate in the close confines of the Mercedes. He'd lost control, raised his voice to her. Years of self-discipline threatened to slip from his grasp.

Covering his face with his hands, he scrubbed at his face. "We'd better get going." Harold and Steven had returned from the mini-mart, and Jason could see them waiting in the white sedan. Starting the engine again, he drove around to the exit, pulling out when he saw Harold behind him.

Ashley reached across the car; he felt the slightest touch of her fingertips on his arm. He shrugged her off. "The subject is closed."

He'd told her what had happened, explained about Steven. He didn't owe her anything more. And he certainly didn't deserve her comfort.

* * *

The mesmerizing drone of tires on pavement lulled Ashley to sleep, but exhaustion kept her there until the Mercedes bumped along up the driveway of the Victorian. Her neck sore from sleeping awkwardly, she tried to stretch out the kinks as Jason pulled up next to her VW in front of the house. Harold continued on toward the back to park beside the guest cottage.

Standing in the living room, still bleary-eyed, she tried to summon the energy to climb the stairs to her bedroom. It was just past ten, a bit early for her to retire for the night. But as tired as she was, she wanted nothing more than to snuggle under the covers and drift off to sleep again. She started for the stairs.

The sound of the back door slamming shut startled her, and she grabbed for the banister. Jason emerged from the kitchen, crossing the living room toward her. It took a moment for her sluggish brain to compute why Jason had come into the house so late at night. When it did, remembering that Harold and Steven were staying in the guest cottage, that Jason would be sleeping in the spare bedroom in the house, all traces of drowsiness vanished from Ashley's mind.

Now completely awake, she stared at him as he drew closer. It had made perfect sense in the car two hours ago that he would use the spare room, but she couldn't wrap her mind around the reality of having him sleeping a couple dozen feet down the hall from her. There was the nursery and a bathroom between them, but what if he got lost in the middle of the night and wandered into her room by mistake?

Even as she realized how ridiculous the notion was,

the fantasy sent a shiver of awareness up her spine. Nearly eight months pregnant with twins, blimplike in proportion, and she still had a sensual awareness of this man who exasperated her and fascinated her in turns.

When she still didn't move, he asked, "Do you need help upstairs?"

"I'm fine." She started up the steps, catching her toe and nearly stumbling. With the extra ballast, recovering her balance wasn't easy—and unnecessary, when Jason's arms encircled her, holding her steady.

"Lean on me," he ordered, wrapping her arm around him. His hand at her waist, he climbed the stairs, his heat soaking into the length of her.

She'd managed to get through the last several weeks without thinking about sex—at least not too much—keeping her thoughts of Jason platonic. But with each new revelation about him—his brother, his harsh, cold stepmother, the tragic death of his mother, empathy softened her feelings toward him; her emotions tangling into incomprehensible feelings she was unwilling to accept.

With any luck, the craziness would disappear once she'd had the babies and her hormones settled down again. Surely, she'd be too preoccupied with taking care of twins to even entertain a naughty thought.

He should have let her go when they reached the landing, but somehow they just kept moving together toward her bedroom. She'd left the door open and a silky knit maternity nightie draped across the rumpled covers. The one morning she'd been too rushed to make the bed, here was Jason, witness to her untidiness.

But it wasn't so much sloppiness that was the problem. The disarray seemed far too inviting. She could all too easily imagine the two of them sliding beneath that thick comforter, between the cool sheets. Jason's warm body would chase that chill away.

Why didn't he let her go? They reached the side of the bed, and Jason turned her toward him. His hand spread over her belly, stroking the taut skin, hot through the knit of her dress. He pulled her closer, head tipped down. His other hand curved around the back of her neck, fingers weaving in her hair.

The heat of his mouth on hers shot through her, stealing her breath. Her heart hammered in her chest, its accelerated beat pounding in her ears. She clutched at his arms, her fingers digging into the sleeves of his sweater, the ribbed wool rasping against her palms.

Every inch of her skin felt sensitized, as if she'd been wrapped in sensual silk. Her breasts felt impossibly heavy, already larger in preparation for birth, they ached for Jason's touch. Her body throbbed between her legs.

His tongue slid inside her mouth, thrusting and tasting. His restless fingers on her belly moved higher, skimming the lower curve of her breast. Her nipple hardened in anticipation.

"I want you." His voice vibrated along her spine like a velvet rasp. "We can't…"

"Just kiss me," she whispered. "Touch me."

Then his thumb skimmed the tightly drawn tip of her breast and she moaned, the sound so low and guttural it shocked her. He stroked again, this time with his palm, circling. Even through the heavy maternity bra, sensation spiraled out from that point, her flesh so responsive, her body strained toward completion.

He must have sensed it. His hand slipped from her neck, grazed along her shoulder, a leisurely path down. His palm still tantalized her breast, skimming the nipple, her body trembling in mounting reaction. His fingers paused at her hip, tightening there briefly before dipping between her legs.

He only had to cup her there, and the lightning jolted between his hands, a sizzling connection that shot her into climax. Moaning, she sagged back against the edge of the bed, her legs barely holding her. Wrapping his arm around her, he eased her back, laying her head on her pillow. He nudged off her shoes, lifting her legs atop the mussed comforter as the last sensual waves washed over her.

Her eyes still shut, she shuddered, holding on to the ebbing sensations. She expected embarrassment would come crashing in, that any moment Jason would turn and walk away, reject her as he had eight months ago. She didn't want to surrender the delight just yet, to watch him go.

She heard his footsteps, soft sounds on the thick carpet, and she waited for the sound of the closing door. But then the bed shifted, rocking slightly. She opened her eyes to see Jason lying on the bed, facing her. The fire in his brown gaze revealed the passion that still burned in him. But mixed with desire, she saw something softer, quieter. She couldn't quite tease it out, couldn't quite decipher what she saw.

Her own heart felt so full she thought it would burst, releasing secrets she wasn't willing to acknowledge. She'd rather hold on to the confusion, persuade herself she didn't know what she was feeling.

He tensed and she knew in another moment he would rise from the bed and leave her. She reached out to him, taking his hand. "Come here," she murmured.

He hesitated briefly before edging closer. She urged him right up next to her, the length of his body pressed alongside hers. There was no mistaking his hard flesh against her hip, his unsatiated arousal. Guilt twinged inside her that he wouldn't experience the satisfaction she had.

But as he cradled her head on his shoulder and draped his other arm across her belly, his breathing steadied. The muscles along his back, usually hard as iron, released bit by bit. When she cupped his cheek with her hand, kissed him lightly on the mouth, he sighed. And for the first time since she'd known him, the tension in him vanished. He lay there vulnerable in her arms, drifting into sleep.

Chapter Twelve

This is what family is like, Ashley thought as she looked around the dinner table. Jason sat at the head of the small dining room table, Ashley to his left and Steven to his right. Harold sat at the other end, regaling them with well-embellished stories of his time in the navy. Steven laughed out loud with a child's abandon, and Jason smiled, truly smiled as Harold stretched his tall tales even taller.

Sara had done her best to make a family life for the two of them, but she'd been run ragged with keeping them fed and clothed. Ashley had spent many long lonely hours by herself, reading, doing homework, dreaming of exactly this kind of scene. These relationships might not be the ones she'd pictured, but the growing closeness, the joy and laughter was real.

Her gaze met Jason's, and his smile softened. Steven's presence these last few weeks had worked a minor miracle. Jason seemed to have found a way to let go of some of the tension he'd gripped so tightly before now. He still guarded himself, kept a subtle distance between them emotionally. But some of the constant pain inside him seemed to have eased.

Paradoxically, as Jason's mood lightened, shadows had gathered in the corners of Ashley's mind. Maybe it was another side effect of the hormonal explosion of pregnancy, or due to having Steven and Harold here, but her dreams had turned dark of late. They'd started the night after they'd brought Steven to Hart Valley—a mélange of images involving her father and mother, Hank Rand's rage and her mother's terrified screams.

Ashley would wake up with her heart racing, groping beside her for Jason. But he wasn't there, hadn't been since that first night. He'd left sometime before she'd woken and they'd never spoken of it. He slept and worked in his room down the hall, and she saw him as little as she had when he'd stayed in the guest cottage.

As Harold finished another story and Steven howled, Ashley rubbed her belly, wishing the two gymnasts inside would quiet down. The two hooligans interrupted the sleep that wasn't disturbed by dreams, using her innards as their own personal bounce house. She'd nearly finished her thirty-fifth week, and while she was just as glad to go as close to full term as possible, she was very ready to see these two born.

Harold rose and started clearing the table. Ashley pushed her chair back. "You cooked, I should clean," she protested.

Harold whisked the plate and flatware from her

place. "I'd say you have a good excuse for being a layabout. Steven can help me. Wash or dry?" he asked Jason's brother.

Ashley sagged back in her seat. "Just as well. I'm about ready to drop."

She and Jason moved to the living room sofa. Through the kitchen door, Steven's and Harold's laughter filtered out as they worked. Jason fixed his gaze on her, his steady focus as palpable as a caress.

Ashley laughed to shake off the tension. "Do I have chicken parmesan on my face?"

He didn't smile. "What happened to your mother?"

The left-field question startled her. "Why do you ask?" She tried to speak casually, but she could barely squeeze out the words.

"I hear you crying at night." He tucked a strand of hair behind her ear. "I go to check on you, and you're talking in your sleep."

His gentle touch only made her want to dissolve into tears. "What am I saying?" she asked, although she could guess.

"You call out for her. Yell at your father to stop. Beg your mother to wake up." His fingers curled into her hair, his voice growing softer. "Did he abuse you?"

She shook her head. "Not me. My mother. And after she died, Sara."

"He hit your sister?" Anger flared in his eyes. "But never you?"

"Once. The night Sara and I ran away."

He traced small circles on her scalp, the sensation melting her bones. "Where is he now?"

"Dead," she said automatically, despite Sara's

recent revelation that he might not be. "In a house fire."

Harold emerged from the kitchen. "Steven wanted to say good-night."

Steven bent to give Ashley a gentle hug. As he often did, Jason walked them out to the cottage, leaving Ashley alone in the silent house for a few minutes.

Sighing, she rested her head on the high sofa back. If she shut her eyes, she'd probably fall asleep. But the bad dreams seemed to loom just beyond the edge of consciousness, dancing with her fears.

Her purse lay on the coffee table, and she tugged it toward her. Buried in her wallet beside the clipping of her dream house was another photograph, this one creased and faded. She fished it out carefully. It was the only tangible reminder Ashley possessed that prevented her mother's face from vanishing from memory.

Ashley gazed down at the picture, her heart filling with love for a woman nearly twenty years dead. Her sister, Sara, had been born with Lucille Rand's dark-auburn hair. Ashley chose to believe her looks and strawberry-blond hair came from some distant relative on her mother's side rather than her monster of a father.

She remembered so little of her mother, just dibs and dabs of well-worn memory. Some had been burnished by Sara, who'd been ten when Lucille died and had a clearer recall. There had been tea parties under the oak tree in the backyard and fantasy vacations to exotic island paradises. Cookies baked for at least one birthday and a small tree at Christmas. Ashley sometimes wondered if these precious, golden moments were real or imaginary.

There was certainly enough horror to drown out the light. Hank Rand's anger sometimes filled every room of the house as he shouted and pounded fists into walls, furniture, her mother's face. Even now, Ashley's stomach contracted with fear.

She heard the back door close and lock, sagging with relief now that Jason was back. She felt safer, more secure with Jason in the house.

As he entered the living room, his gaze fell to the photograph in her hand. She turned it toward him. "That's her. My mother."

He held the small rectangle carefully. "You look just like her."

She couldn't suppress a smile of pleasure. "Sara took after her more."

Studying the photo another moment, he glanced up at her. "I don't think so. You've got her eyes, her mouth." His attention shifted to Ashley's mouth, and a shiver tingled up her spine.

"It's all I have left of her. We were lucky to get that when we left." That memory was all too vivid. "We had to sneak out while my father was passed out from drinking. When I realized I'd forgotten the photograph, I begged Sara to go back in for it. She was nearly in the clear when he woke up. He chased us down the street as we drove away in his car."

Now he scrutinized the photo again. "Can I keep this a couple of days?"

"It's my only copy."

"I'll be careful with it." He looked up at her. "I promise I won't mess it up."

For an instant she could see the little boy in his

face, promising to be good. As careful as he was with her, she knew he would protect her only keepsake of her mother. "Sure."

He turned to an antique writing desk in the corner of the living room and withdrew an envelope. Slipping the photo inside, he tucked the envelope in his shirt pocket.

He reached for her. "I'll take you upstairs."

She linked her fingers with his. "Why do you want the photograph?"

"I'll tell you later."

She'd have to be satisfied with that. He walked her up the stairs and to her room. He lingered with her by the bed, leaning in to kiss her. A soft brush of his mouth against hers, his lips warm and inviting. She would have given anything to have him sleep with her tonight, to maybe keep the dreams at bay. But she couldn't bring herself to ask.

He drew back, his hands still holding hers. "What happened to her, Ashley?"

Rage. Screams. "She died."

"How?" he pressed.

"What does it matter?" she asked, although she knew it mattered greatly.

"When you talk in your sleep," he said, sweeping a wisp of hair back from her brow, "you're so scared."

She was terrified now. She'd always rejected her suspicions as unreliable memory, but her recent dreams had her doubting herself.

She struggled to hold on to the story her father told, the one even Sara believed. "She fell. Down the stairs."

He curved his hand around her cheek. "Did you see?"

"Yes. No…" She did remember her mother at the bottom of the steps, her body broken. But another image intruded, of her father yelling at her, ordering her into her room. And she'd run, the sound of his shouted threats chasing her to the dubious safety of her room.

Jason put his arms around her, holding her tightly against him. She had to fight tears, so much harder to hold back with the ebb and flow of hormones swirling through her. She might not love him, but Jason had become a rock, a foundation for her. She was grateful to have him with her.

Letting her go, he started for the door, then paused there. "No one will ever hurt you again, Ashley. I'll make sure of it."

He walked out, his footsteps receding down the hall. As she turned to the empty bed, she again wished she'd had the courage to ask him to stay with her. But knowing he was nearby would have to be enough.

Thanksgiving at Sara's house was more raucous than usual, with twelve crowded around the table—Sara's small family of three, Ashley, Jason and his brother, and assorted Hart Valley "strays" who didn't have a place to be that day. Harold had gone back east to celebrate the holiday with his daughter despite Steven's begging him to stay.

The strays included nine-year-old Grace, a former student at Sara's Rescued Hearts Riding School and Grace's mother, Alicia. An ebullient little girl, Grace chattered a mile a minute, asking Ashley a million questions about the babies-to-be and enthusiastically volunteering to babysit anytime.

Unfortunately, Sara's delicious dinner had been wasted on Ashley. She'd felt out of sorts all day, her back aching, her stomach in a knot as the twins seemed to do their best to squeeze aside every internal organ but the one they occupied. She could swear they were battling it out inside her, which didn't bode well for future sibling relations.

She sucked in her breath at a stabbing pain in her lower back. Jason immediately focused on her. "What is it?"

She rubbed at her back. "I think I overdid it cleaning my classroom yesterday."

"I told you to wait. Steven and I would have done it for you."

"I thought I could—ouch."

She must have cried out more loudly than she'd intended because suddenly Sara's attention zeroed on her from the other side of the noisy table. "What's going on, Ashley?" she called out above the din.

"It's nothing. It's just my back."

But everyone was staring at her now, Grace wide-eyed, Steven grinning, her brother-in-law, Keith, with a bemused smile. Another pain dug into her back, then to her complete mortification, she wet herself all over Sara's dining-room chair.

It took her a moment to realize that what had happened was nothing to be ashamed of. She groped for Jason's hand and gasped out, "I think my water broke."

A moment later pandemonium broke out, the ruckus barely kept in check by Sara. "Jason, get her to the car. Is her suitcase in the trunk?"

Jason looked as frantic as Ashley had ever seen him. "Not yet. I thought we had time."

"Pull yourself together, Jason," Sara snapped. "Keith, go pick up Ashley's bag."

Ashley was about to tell them where to find it, but another pain shot up her back. Grimacing, she gripped Jason's hand even tighter.

He didn't even flinch. "The suitcase is in the coat closet downstairs."

Easing her from the chair, he supported her on one side while Sara took the other. "At least you're only five minutes from the hospital. If you'd been home it would have been more like twenty."

As they hustled her through the house and out onto the porch, Ashley gasped out, "Teddy bear."

Sara put a hand to Ashley's forehead. "The labor's making her crazy."

"It's her focus object," Jason clarified.

"Hang on, Keith!" Sara called out, then turned to Ashley. "Where is it?"

Too dazed by pain to remember, Ashley just shook her head. Somehow they'd reached the Mercedes and Jason gently set her inside. "Don't worry. I've got you. Don't worry, honey."

The pain must have wreaked havoc with her mind. She had to be hallucinating Jason's tender tone, his endearment.

When he climbed into the car beside her, he thrust something in her hand. It was the photo of her mother, laminated and attached to a keychain. Just seeing her mother's smiling face softened the pain, gentled the spasms of her body.

The tires spit gravel as they gunned away from Keith and Sara's house. Jason brushed her arm with his fingertips. "Will the picture be okay?"

She nodded, clutching it tighter as another wave

rolled over her. "Thank you," she managed when it had passed.

Jason stomped harder on the accelerator.

He'd never been so terrified in his life. Ashley beside him in the car, her fingers digging into his arm, the rush to the hospital with his sweat-slick hands slipping on the wheel, the frantic moments when he thought he'd made a wrong turn and wouldn't get them there in time.

But then there was the hospital, its bright lights illuminating the way. And nurses waiting with a gurney in the parking lot. He sent a silent thank-you to Sara, who no doubt had phoned ahead to prepare them.

Although the twins had seemed in a tremendous rush to be born at Sara's and on their way to the hospital, they turned stubborn once they had Ashley safely inside just after 7:00 p.m. Her labor slowed, a relief to Jason who couldn't stand to see Ashley's agony. But Ashley made it clear she was eager to be done with the process, and when the wrenching labor speeded up again four hours later, she bore it with fortitude.

He'd never seen anyone so courageous. When Steven had first woken from his coma twenty years ago, had struggled back into the world, fighting for whatever mental capacity he could grasp, Jason had been awed by his bravery. But Ashley stunned him, too. When the pain consumed her, she just held him tighter, her gaze fixed on the photograph he kept in view for her. Her valor filled him with an unexpected, overwhelming emotion.

Then he caught his first glimpse of his daughter, and pure, undistilled joy burst inside him. From the sound of her first squall to the indignant expression on her ruddy face, she enchanted him. With the birth of his son moments later, he thought his heart would rocket from his chest.

Entering the world at just after midnight Thanksgiving night, Meredith Lucille had weighed in at just under five pounds, Marshall Kenneth at five pounds one ounce. A few weeks early, their lungs were fine—a fact that Meredith liked to confirm at every opportunity.

They'd settled Ashley and the babies in her room around two in the morning, and she'd immediately fallen asleep. Jason had dozed fitfully in one of the hard plastic hospital chairs at the foot of the bed. Each time he woke, his gaze immediately sought out Ashley, then the babies, still grappling with the truth of these new lives.

As late-fall rain slapped against the window, the sky already darkening at 4:00 p.m., the babies slept in their bassinets set up on either side of Ashley's bed. After nursing them in turn, Ashley had drifted off into a well-deserved nap. Jason still sat in his chair, sore and bleary-eyed, watching over them.

The babies had needed a bottle-feeding at one point, when Ashley was just too exhausted to cope with nursing. They'd offered to let him feed Meredith and Marshall, but he didn't trust himself yet to safely hold the infants. Despite the books he'd read, the pages of information he'd downloaded from the Internet, he feared he'd somehow hurt them.

That he ached to feel that sweet weight in his arms shocked him. He'd always thought that kind of immediate connection was restricted to mothers, an extension of the physical link during pregnancy. But he felt so fiercely protective of these tiny people who slept in their bassinets, he knew there was nothing he wouldn't do for them.

How could he leave them? How could he move back to San José, go back to his old life, pretend they didn't exist? It would be as painful as walking away from Steven, institutionalizing him as Maureen had insisted years ago. Jason's father had flatly refused—he'd had at least that much compassion in him. Jason could no more turn his back on these twins than he could leave his brother with strangers.

But what the hell did he know about caring for babies? If they lived with him, they'd be raised by nannies, not him. He was terrified to hold them, what made him think he could give them proper care? They'd be better off with Ashley as he'd agreed weeks ago.

But I can't leave them. The realization pounded inside him.

"Hey."

Her quiet voice tugged his attention from his dark thoughts. "Hey."

"Did you hear? We can go home tomorrow." She smiled, and warmth spread inside him.

He wanted so badly to be close to her, even here in the hospital just a few hours after she'd given birth. He had to resist the impulse to stretch out in the narrow bed beside her and pull her into his arms, to just hold her. "The baby seats are in the car."

"Good." Her fingers pleated the thin hospital blanket. "I wanted to thank you."

"For what?"

"You were there, Jason. When I needed you…"

"I said I would."

"Yes. You did." She shifted in the bed, wincing a little. "But you followed through."

"Your sister would have done a better job."

"I didn't want my sister there," she said firmly. "I wanted you."

He didn't know what to say to that, didn't know how to cope with the emotions brewing inside him. He looked at Meredith to Ashley's right, then at Marshall snuggled in his bassinet on the other side. "Ashley," he rasped out, "what am I going to do?"

His whispered plea hung in the air between them. Ashley tried to decipher the pain sharpening his face, the anguish in his eyes. But as usual with Jason, nothing was clear.

Moving slowly, mindful of how sore she was, she pushed herself upright. "Talk to me, Jason."

He rose and moved to stand over Marshall's bassinet. "I wasn't supposed to feel this way."

"Yes, you are," she said softly. "You're their father."

"It's not enough. Nothing I've ever done in my life has been enough."

She took his hand. "You helped me create these miracles."

"But what good am I to them?" He laughed harshly. "I'm afraid to hold them. I'll do something wrong. I'll hurt them."

"You think I'm not scared I'll mess up? That's every parent's fear."

"It would be better to just walk away." His hand tightening in hers, he stared down at Marshall. "For them. For you."

That was what she wanted, wasn't it? To have him gone, to raise these babies on her own. Then why was her heart breaking at the thought of it?

Sliding her legs out of the way, she tugged his hand. "Sit down."

He hesitated before easing himself next to her. Pulling Marshall's bassinet a little closer, she lifted the warm bundle from it, cradled him in her arms for a moment. Pressing a kiss to Marshall's cheek, she held him out to Jason. "Hold your son."

Real fear sparked in his face. "No."

Marshall balanced against her, she crooked Jason's arm. "Yes."

Before he could move away, she popped the baby into the safety of his father's embrace. Positioning Jason's other arm to give him a more secure hold, she folded back the blanket to give them both a better view of the tiny infant.

As he snuggled him close, the fear in Jason's eyes faded, replaced slowly by a remarkable elation. Steadying Marshall on his arm, Jason rose, his thumb stroking the small cheek.

"He's perfect. How could I have made anything so perfect?"

Joy spilled out from Ashley's heart and tears pricked her eyes. She'd blamed her emotions on the pregnancy, and no doubt what she was feeling now was the aftermath of giving birth. But somehow, Jason had crept inside her, day by day, bit by bit, and she knew she would never be able to dislodge him.

It was simple affection, surely. The way he doted over his son, seeing his adoration, his gentleness had moved her. And his kindness toward his brother, his patience with Zak in her classroom, had shown her a side of Jason she might never have suspected existed in the hard-driven young businessman. Her feelings went no further than that.

Her gaze locked with his and alarm nibbled at her. What if he saw something in her eyes that he misconstrued, misinterpreted as more than affection. Even still, she couldn't seem to pull away, too enthralled by his intensity as his son slept in his arms.

He moved closer to her, and her heart reacted with a double-time beat. "Marry me, Ashley."

Her wayward thoughts pushed the ridiculous question out of her mouth. "Do you love me?"

He didn't answer, didn't have to. She saw it in his eyes.

She would have said no. Intended to. But then Meredith woke, squalling like an angry cat and setting off her brother. For the moment, marriage and love took a backseat to hungry babies.

Chapter Thirteen

"You said you wouldn't marry him," Sara said, disapproval clear in her face as she cradled her five-month-old son, Evan.

Ashley repositioned week-old Marshall in her lap as he nursed enthusiastically. "I haven't said yes yet."

At her feet, Meredith napped on a thick comforter on Sara's living room floor. The little girl made kissy faces as she dreamed, no doubt contemplating her turn at her mother's breast. She'd likely wake just as Ashley finished with Marshall.

His legs pumping like a cyclist's, Evan wriggled in Sara's arms. She took a tighter hold on her wiggly son. "But you're going to."

She forced a smile. "Do I have a choice?"

"Of course you do." Sara's gaze narrowed on her. "Is he threatening to fight for custody?"

"He just wants to be part of their lives. We both do." She stroked Marshall's baby-soft cheek. "Marriage really does seem like the best solution."

Still struggling for freedom, Evan let out a squawk. Sara set her son on the floor. "Except you don't love him."

Ashley dropped her gaze, uncomfortable with her own evasiveness. "Of course I don't. What does that matter?"

"Oh, Ashley." Sara put her arms around her. "I want you to have what I have. A man that loves you."

It was what Ashley had hoped for all these years. "Sometimes life doesn't quite work out the way you expect."

Sara drew back, tipping up Ashley's chin to meet her gaze. "I'm behind you, no matter what. You know that, don't you?"

Keeping her eyes steady on Sara, Ashley nodded. "Of course."

"If you want to marry him…"

Ashley swallowed past a lump in her throat. "I truly think it would be best." Then Meredith called out, saving Ashley from any further discussion.

Later, with the twins strapped safely in the backseat of the Camry Jason had insisted on giving her, Ashley drove home, mulling over her conversation with her sister. As much as Ashley might have wanted that one true love—the kind of relationship Sara shared with her husband—wouldn't what she'd have with Jason be just as good? She'd come to respect him, care for him; she liked to think that to the extent he could, Jason felt the same. How much further along the road was it to love, anyway?

She knew how far; her heart sensed it. Ached for it, longed for it. She was only fooling herself to think otherwise.

He'd be a devoted father and a faithful husband. He'd come home to her every night, give her anything she needed.

As long as what she needed wasn't his love. And if she had even the least modicum of self-preservation, she'd keep her heart tightly locked up. She'd pour her love out to Marshall and Meredith, give to them until she couldn't give anymore. Because the moment she opened that door to Jason, she would be lost.

Despair threatened, hovering over her like a dark cloud. She needed to be practical, to think of the twins. They'd have a much better life with both a mother and father raising them. For her to expect more would just be selfish.

She was surprised to see Jason's car in front of the Victorian when she pulled up the drive. He'd gone into the Bay Area yesterday and she'd thought he wouldn't be back until late tonight. He must have been watching for her because he stepped out onto the front porch as she parked the Camry. A dangerous happiness welled up inside her upon seeing him, wiping away the despair.

She waited until he'd unstrapped Meredith from her car seat and she had Marshall in her arms. The diaper bag would just have to wait. "Jason," she called as he turned toward the house.

He waited, his expression expectant. Meredith snuggled against his neck, and Ashley's heart filled with love. For Meredith. For her and not for Jason.

"Yes," she told him. "I'll marry you."

* * *

The rain pounded down on the day of the wedding, as if the skies grieved for their loveless union. The Sunday ceremony a week before Christmas wasn't quite what Ashley had imagined as a young girl when she'd dreamed of marriage. But the recitation of their vows in the parlor of the Hart Valley Inn was nice enough, thanks to the bridal gown Sara had lent her and the incredible food Beth Henley, the inn owner, had provided.

The handful of guests that fit easily into the inn's small dining room had enjoyed the coq au vin, Caesar salad and crusty sourdough rolls Beth had served. She'd offered them use of the ballroom for dancing, but Ashley thought that would make it seem too much like a real wedding. The license they'd signed after the ceremony might be legal and binding, but as she sat there after dinner in Sara's borrowed dress, Ashley felt like the world's biggest fraud.

With Evan on her hip, Sara sat next to Ashley at the now-cleared dining table. "Tell me you're really okay with this."

"I'm fine," Ashley lied, her gaze on Jason across the room.

Over by the fireplace, Jason and Harold each cradled an infant, Steven between them doting over his new nephews. Harold, a godsend these three weeks since the twins' birth, held Marshall. Jason snuggled Meredith in his arms, bending his head to kiss her tiny nose.

His kiss during the ceremony had been just as chaste, the barest brush across her mouth. She'd wanted to hold him there, feel his warmth, have him taste her. But he'd let her go quickly.

Even now she felt the loss. Would it have been so terrible if he'd given her a real kiss?

She felt Sara's gaze on her. Ashley turned to her sister. "What?"

Sara scrutinized her, her expression serious. "I think it's time you got out of that dress."

"Yes, please." On her feet, Ashley tried to straighten the too-tight bodice. "I'm about to split a seam. I think I've kissed size six goodbye."

"You haven't, but believe me, I'm enjoying being smaller than you for once." Sara nudged her into motion.

As they cut through the parlor, Sara transferred Evan into his father's care. Climbing the stairs, they headed for the room Beth had set aside for them to change.

Sara turned Ashley's back toward her and started in on the row of buttons. "I thought you said you didn't love him."

Ashley yanked away. "I don't."

Sara stared at her, her eyes narrowing. With a not-too-gentle spin, she turned Ashley around again and continued unfastening. "I don't know what's worse… knowingly entering into a loveless marriage or marrying a man you love who doesn't love you back."

Ashley couldn't help it; she stiffened under her sister's ministrations. She forced herself to relax. "Sara, this isn't any of your business."

She could feel Sara's ire as her fingers fumbled with the round buttons. "It is when you're hurting."

"Sara, I'm fine—"

"I'm not an idiot!" Sara's angry tug popped a button off the dress. It skittered across the floor and under the bureau.

Inexplicable tears tightened Ashley's throat. She knew she had to keep them at bay, to hide the truth not just from Sara but from herself. But when Sara turned Ashley around to face her, there was no holding back the emotion.

With Sara's arms around her, Ashley sobbed, tears spilling from her eyes, her heart in tatters. She hadn't felt as lost since her mother died.

"Oh, sweetheart," Sara murmured.

"What…am I…going to do?" Ashley stuttered between sobs.

"We'll figure it out," Sara said soothingly.

Ashley pulled back. "How do I stop feeling this way?"

It was the kind of question she might have asked her big sister as a child. But Ashley knew she wouldn't get an answer.

Sara stroked back Ashley's hair. "I don't suppose he loves you."

Ashley dropped her gaze. It would hurt too much to see her sister's pity. "I think he cares for me in his own way. Like he does Steven."

"Maybe in time—"

"He won't." Ashley looked into her sister's face. "I don't think he can. There's something missing in him, Sara."

"He's a man. It might be buried deep, but he still feels it."

"Maybe he did once." Sorrow cut at Ashley. "I don't know if he can anymore."

Sara's smile didn't reach her eyes. She gave Ashley another hug, then finished unbuttoning the dress. Ashley changed into slacks and a sweater, then she fished the round white button out from under the bureau. Ashley insisted on keeping the dress so she could repair the torn button loop and get it cleaned.

Back downstairs they rushed the cutting of the wedding cake when the twins got cranky, Meredith as usual leading the way with her full-throated wails. Within an hour after dinner, they'd packed up the gifts and the leftover cake and headed up to the Victorian. There Ashley nursed the twins while Sara and Keith lingered over coffee.

An hour later, company gone, the twins in their cribs, Jason out in the guest cottage with Harold and Steven, Ashley shut herself in her bedroom. The sight of Sara's simple white wedding dress laid across the bed set off an ache inside her. As reality took hold of her, she sank onto the foot of the bed and dropped her head in her hands.

What had she done? Why hadn't she done a better job of guarding her heart? The roller coaster of pregnancy and childbirth had simply thrown her for a loop, had wrenched her from one emotional extreme to another. She'd had no real defense against Jason.

She heard the back door slam shut, heard his footsteps on the stairs. Swiping away tears with the heel of her palm, she picked up Sara's dress and hung it in the closet. With any luck, Jason would just walk on by her room.

But her luck had died a bitter death that day. He rapped on her door, called out, "Ashley?"

She could pretend to be asleep, or in the bathroom. But she could imagine him there, waiting for her to answer. She couldn't bring herself to ignore him.

She opened the door, crossing her arms over her middle, as if she could somehow protect herself from the pain. "I'm tired, Jason."

"I just wanted to say good-night."

He still wore his wedding clothes, the placket of the white dress shirt stained with something one of the babies must have left, the tie gone but the carnation still pinned to his jacket. As rumpled as he was, he looked entirely perfect.

She longed to pull him inside. Instead she made to shut the door. "Good night."

His toe caught the door before she could close it. Pushing it open again, he pulled her into his arms. She didn't put up an ounce of resistance when his mouth covered hers.

There was nothing chaste about this kiss. His tongue dove in immediately, thrusting between her lips in an invasion she welcomed, craved. As his tongue dueled with hers, explored her mouth, heat shot through her, a line of sensation sizzling up her spine.

One hand behind her head, the other pushed against the small of her back, he melded her body to his. She felt the hard ridge of him through his slacks, and she longed to cup her hand over him, to stroke that length, send him into ecstasy.

Ready to drag him over to the bed, she moaned in frustration when he pulled away from her. Fire burning in his dark eyes, he rasped out, "How long?"

She struggled to understand what he was asking. "I don't—"

He caressed her cheek with an impatient hand. "When can we make love?"

His brusque tone doused the conflagration inside her. She wasn't even sure why. She wanted him as much as he wanted her. She knew he hadn't married her just for access to her body. But knowing how she felt about him, that he couldn't return her love wiped away desire.

She backed away until he dropped his hands. "We never agreed to sex."

"You're right. We didn't. I just thought…" He shook his head. "Sorry. My mistake."

He slammed the door hard enough that Ashley feared it had wakened the twins. But not a sound emerged from the baby monitor, so she had nothing to distract her from the waves of pain radiating through her.

What would it hurt if they made love? She knew the answer to that—she'd tie her heart even more securely to him. That exquisite intimacy would be the final knot she would never untangle.

But how could she walk away from that paradise? Why not just enjoy the physical, allow herself to pretend in those moments that he felt the same about her as she did about him? Could her heart be broken any more than it was already?

God save her, she wanted whatever crumbs she could get from him. Even if it was only the passion of his body, even if it would eventually leave her empty.

Resolute, she left her room and started down the hall. She stopped short when she saw the babies' door open, glimpsed Jason inside next to Marshall's crib.

Stunned at the naked emotion in Jason's face, she stood silent in the doorway watching him. This wasn't affection or caring or a father's protectiveness. This was love, pure and powerful. He loved that baby boy and the infant girl in the other crib with just as much intensity as Ashley did.

Even if he never felt the same about her, if he never

responded in kind to her devotion, that he could love, wasn't that enough? A marriage could survive on less.

When he looked up at her, he didn't immediately hide what he felt for Marshall behind the usual mask. He gave her entry to that corner of himself for an instant, unashamed. Then something clicked and the light went out.

He walked toward her, his expression neutral. Ashley pulled him from the room.

"Three more weeks," she told him, holding his hand until she was sure he understood. Then she returned to her room where she cried herself to sleep.

Three days before Christmas, Ashley packed up the twins in the Camry, and with Harold beside her and Steven crammed between the car seats in the back, she drove out to one of the local tree farms. Jason begged off, saying he had to work.

With Meredith tucked in Ashley's baby carrier and Marshall in Harold's, they hiked the hillside, Steven running on ahead in search of the perfect tree. Never having the space in the small dorm rooms and shared houses during her college years, Ashley hadn't had a real Christmas tree in years. She'd always spent the holiday with Sara, anyway, so buying her own tree hadn't made sense.

But this year, despite the delay caused by the twins' birth and the wedding, she was bound and determined to have a tree in her own house. Sara contributed extra ornaments she hadn't used and purchased a few more as early Christmas gifts. They'd string popcorn and cranberries this afternoon as a finishing touch.

Winded, Ashley stopped to lean against a tall red-wood. "How long have you been with the Kerrigans?" she asked Harold.

"I've been Steven's caretaker nearly twenty years," the older man told her. "But I've known the family longer than that."

"Did you know Steven before…"

"Before the accident? Yes." He looked through the tangle of silvertips and Douglas fir to where Steven wandered amongst the trees. "The first Mrs. Kerrigan befriended me when my wife died. After twenty-five years of marriage…I had a hard time letting go."

A gust of wind cut past them, sending a winter chill through Ashley's heavy sweater. She tucked Meredith's blanket more securely around her. "What was she like?"

"The first Mrs. Kerrigan?" Harold smiled. "Mary was the kindest, most gentle woman you would ever want to meet. She loved both her boys, but the way she stood up for Jason…"

"Stood up for him…?"

"At school. Jason was…an active little boy in the classroom. No matter how hard he tried, he couldn't sit still. He had so much energy, he'd get up and pace around the room."

Ashley immediately understood, seeing how well Jason handled the hyperactive Zak, knowing that the boy would work better in motion. "I gather the teacher didn't appreciate that."

As mild-mannered as Harold was, the flash of anger in his face surprised Ashley. "She reprimanded him a dozen times a day. When the other students tormented him for being different, she didn't do a thing to stop it."

"Some educators find it hard to handle special-needs kids," Ashley said, trying to feel charitable toward Jason's long-ago teacher.

"This woman should never have been in a classroom." Harold adjusted the baby carrier on his chest, giving little Marshall a kiss on the head. "She wanted all her students in orderly rows. She couldn't handle a boy as bright as Jason."

Her heart ached for him, brilliant but impulsive, his mind firing off ideas he couldn't find words to express. Now the time they'd shared as tutors at Berkeley made even more sense. He'd always hooked up with the active kids, the ones who tore through classrooms, who jumped from one concept to the next, sometimes skipping steps in the process that other, more conventional, students might have to take. Most of the tutors who worked with them threw up their hands at students like that, unable to see inside them the way Jason did.

"What happened with Jason's teacher?" Ashley asked.

"Mary went down there like an avenging angel. Told the principal that if the teacher didn't have the imagination to teach her son, he'd better find another one who did." Harold laughed. "When Mary got het up, she was a force to be reckoned with."

Ashley wished she could have seen her. "And then?"

"The principal moved Jason to another classroom. To a more sympathetic teacher who could handle his energy." Sorrow lined Harold's face. "That was the last year Mary was alive."

And Jason lost his only champion. Considering how little he spoke of his father, not to mention what a harpy his stepmother was, Ashley could imagine how adrift, how abandoned Jason must have felt after his mother died. How many more teachers had come along, dismissing him as just a badly behaved little boy, no one to stand beside him, stand up for him?

Nearly out of sight down the hillside, Steven called out to them, "I found one!"

He waved his arms, jumping with excitement. Ashley and Harold started toward him, walking carefully on the uneven ground thick with pine and fir needles. Harold helped her around a fallen log, holding a stout redwood to keep his balance.

When they'd cleared the other side, he kept his hand on her arm, stopping her forward progress. "I want you to understand…Jason wasn't always like this."

"What do you mean?" she asked, although she had an inkling of what he was talking about.

"He wasn't always so hard. So cold. Holding himself apart from others."

"Sometimes I catch glimpses of a different man." But so seldom. And so fleeting.

"He used to bring his mother flowers. Usually a prized specimen pulled from some neighbor's yard." Harold chuckled, then grew more serious. "Sometimes the flowers came with a note. After his name, the first words he learned to write were 'I love you.'"

That took the air out of her lungs. She was glad of Harold's hand on her arm. "You know he blames himself for her death."

His lips compressed. "That's his father's doing. I know Ken was hurting with his wife dead, Steven injured, the baby lost—"

"The baby?"

"Hey!" Steven waved at them again. "Come on, guys!"

Harold gave her arm a squeeze. "I've said enough. You'll have to talk to Jason about that."

Then he continued down the hill, glancing back to be sure she followed, leaving her with another secret left concealed.

Three days later on Christmas morning, a cold front closed in, bringing a rare snowfall to the Sierra foothills. Only a few inches, it was enough to blanket the ground with white—icing on top of a joyful day.

Jason had bought a gleaming gold-plated ornament for each of the twins, engraving their names above the year and the inscription "Baby's First Christmas." They hung side by side on the eight-foot tree at eye level where Steven had placed them. Jason had also managed to unearth two similar baubles after a quick trip back to San José, the two tarnished gold disks also proclaiming a first Christmas, but for Jason and Steven. Ashley made sure they were placed on the tree beside Meredith's and Marshall's.

Ashley's last-minute shopping trip earlier in the week had been a challenge with the twins, but with Sara's assistance, she'd managed to find some Disney DVDs for Steven and a lovely Irish wool sweater for Harold. She'd agonized over what to buy Jason, finally settling on a couple sweaters and a stack of science fiction books Harold was sure he'd enjoy.

After they'd stuffed themselves with Harold's pancakes and sausages, Steven had volunteered to distribute the presents around the living room. With Jason beside her on the sofa and Harold opposite them on the recliner, Ashley watched with bemusement as her pile grew. After so many Christmases with her father when she and Sara received nothing, they'd always tried to give each other as many little gifts as they could afford. But the tower of brightly wrapped boxes beside her outstripped their most prosperous holiday haul.

Even the twins, keeping each other company in a playpen in the middle of the living room, had a tidy stack of presents. Seeing their number, Ashley suspected she wasn't the only one to succumb to the temptation to purchase toys and clothes the babies were still too young to use.

The last gift removed from under the tree, Steven called to Jason, "Should I go get it now?"

A quick glance at Ashley, then Jason nodded. "Just be careful. Remember it's breakable."

Steven hurried out the back door toward the guest cottage. Ashley had already seen several tags on her pile with Steven's name scrawled as the giver, so she wondered what the big surprise might be. When he returned, bearing a large flat rectangle almost reverently, her curiosity grew.

Steven placed it in her hands, making sure she had a good grip before he let go. "That's from Jason."

Under the festive Christmas paper, she could feel what seemed to be a picture frame. Had he secretly taken a photo of the twins and had it framed? Or maybe it was one of the wedding pictures, blown up as a keepsake. She smiled at the thought of such a sweet gesture.

She asked Jason, "Can I open this?"

She saw wariness in his gaze. No doubt he worried she might not like the present. "Go ahead," he told her.

Turning it over, she hooked her fingers under the edge of the paper and tore. She saw from the back that her guess had been correct—it was a framed picture. Easing off the rest of the wrapping paper, she hesitated before flipping it over, wanting to draw out the anticipation. If it was the twins, she guessed Marshall would be grinning his baby grin, but likely Meredith would be scowling.

She turned the picture over. And for a moment she couldn't breathe.

It wasn't Marshall and Meredith, nor one of the digital snapshots Sara had taken at their wedding.

It was her mother. That same creased and folded photo that was her only remembrance of a woman she'd loved so dearly. That one smiling image that had kept her alive all these years in Ashley's heart. Except all the creases were gone. The color had been restored, the picture now as vivid as the day it had been taken.

Ashley had thought when Jason had borrowed the photo he only meant to have it laminated for her to protect it. She'd had no idea he'd do this for her.

"How did you get the creases out?" She ran her fingers lightly over the glass. "How did you make the color so bright?"

"I had one of my technicians scan it," he told her. "Then she enhanced the image on a computer. I gave her a photograph of you to work with."

She could barely take a breath for the tightness in her throat. "Sara's picture would have been better."

"No," Jason said quietly. "Look at the eyes. Her mouth. You could be her twin."

The tears spilled over, running down her cheeks,

wetting her face. She swiped them away, but more fell, a torrent of emotion.

She felt Jason's hand taking hers. "Is it okay?" he asked, uncertainty in his tone. "Was it the wrong thing to do? I wasn't sure if you—"

Setting aside the portrait, she threw her arms around him. "It's perfect. It's the best present you ever could have given me." She barely got the words out before she sobbed again.

He rubbed her back, his strong hands soothing. "Good. I'm glad."

I love you! she called out in her mind as she clung to him. *I love you.*

She longed to make the declaration out loud, yearned to hear him answer in kind. But wisdom held her silent.

Chapter Fourteen

As she waited for Jason to finish a call upstairs before her one-o'clock six-week checkup, Ashley nursed Marshall on the living room sofa while Sara sat beside her with Meredith. The demanding Meredith had already had her turn and now she lay propped on her aunt's shoulder, content for the moment.

"I really appreciate you taking them for the afternoon," Ashley told her sister.

"So you said." Sara gave Meredith a pat.

Ashley could see the curiosity in her sister's eyes about why she needed a sitter, but she wasn't about to satisfy it. "Harold took Steven into Sacramento to tour the capitol, so I couldn't leave the twins with him."

"I'm glad to do it. Keith is working at home today, so he can give me a hand with the triple terrors."

Marshall had drifted off to sleep, so Ashley set him on her lap to adjust her bra and sweater. Jason's conversation filtered from upstairs, the sound of his voice stroking her nerves. She couldn't make out what he was saying, but somehow everything these past two weeks had an erotic weight to them. The anticipation leading up to her six-week checkup had in turns filled her with fear and excitement.

Ashley fitted Marshall to her shoulder and gently patted his back. "We might as well get them into the car."

They'd switched the infant seats to Sara's sedan earlier. Grabbing the diaper bag on her way out the front door, Ashley walked her sister out. She felt a little wrench in her middle as she tucked Marshall into his seat. This would be her first time away from the twins in six weeks. She'd already started transitioning them to the bottle in preparation for returning to her classroom in the middle of February. She wasn't sure how she'd cope being away from them for the hours she worked.

After Sara drove away, Ashley lingered in the front yard, reluctant to return to the charged atmosphere of the house. If Jason hadn't come downstairs yet, she wasn't about to go up to tell him it was time to leave. He still slept in the room he'd made his office, and any connection between Jason and beds started her imagination working overtime. If she let her mind run in that direction, they'd never make it to her checkup.

Maybe she'd just go grab her purse and wait for Jason on the front porch. The porch swing might soothe her jangled nerves and give her something to think about besides Jason and beds and what would happen after her visit to the doctor's.

But as she stepped inside the front door, she ran right into Jason's arms. She clutched at him for balance, his cashmere sweater soft under her hands, his shoulders powerful. Without even meaning to, she eased closer, her hips against his. As she pressed against him, she realized she wasn't the only one with a wandering mind this morning.

His gaze had fixed on her mouth, and she had to struggle to breathe, just contemplating him kissing her. "You'd better not," she gasped out.

His gaze lifted to hers, his eyes burning with heat. "Where are the twins?"

"Gone with Sara. She'll keep them until dinnertime."

"We should go, then." He didn't move. Unless you counted that pressure of his hips toward her.

With an effort Ashley let him go. "Let me get my purse."

Thankfully, he waited outside. She was so rattled, she couldn't immediately remember where she'd left her small leather bag. It took her a full minute to locate it under a rumpled baby blanket.

Jason had the car running. Although Dr. Karpoor kept an office in Hart Valley, every Friday she worked in her Marbleville clinic. That stretched out the time it would take to get the all-clear, then return home. Ashley was certain she'd go mad before then.

Jason locked up and helped her down the stairs, a habit he hadn't let go of since her pregnancy. Touching him wasn't the best idea; it drove reason and logic entirely out of her mind. But sitting in the car beside him with no physical contact between them, she reacted even more strongly to him. Her fantasies of the warmth of his skin, his fingers stroking her, spun out of control.

Jason stayed in the waiting room during Dr. Karpoor's brief exam. With the doctor's confirmation that she had healed nicely and could resume normal activities, Ashley dressed and returned to the waiting room. She found Jason pacing along the corridor outside the medical office complex. He spotted her, hurrying toward her before the office door shut behind her. He slipped his arm around her, and they walked together toward the parking lot.

"We can stop for lunch," he said as he pulled out of the lot. "Unless you already ate."

"I haven't." Her stomach rebelled at the thought of food.

"Then we can—"

"No. Let's go home."

His hands strangled the steering wheel as he turned onto the interstate. He'd pushed up the sleeves of his sweater despite the January chill, and she could see the muscles and tendons working in his arms.

She wanted to reach for him, to touch him everywhere. To watch his response to her. She forced herself to face forward, gripped her hands in her lap.

The car had barely rolled to a stop in the driveway of the Victorian before he killed the engine. Too impatient to wait for him, she climbed from the car and rounded it as he did, meeting him halfway. His arms enfolded her in an instant, his mouth covering hers, hot and insistent.

She would gladly have had him take her right there, on the hood of the car. In that moment she didn't even care what kind of scandal it would cause in town.

One last hot thrust of his tongue and Jason tugged away, grabbing her hand to lead her toward the house. He fumbled the key twice when he tried to unlock the door, then managed it with trembling hands. Once he'd shut the door behind them, he pressed her against it, his hands exploring her body, from hip to breast.

"Upstairs," he said. "Not here."

She moaned in protest, but he took her hand again to lead her through the living room and up the stairs, kissing, touching along the way. At her bedroom door, he released her. "Wait here," he told her before striding down the hall to his own room.

When he returned, he backed her into her bedroom, trailing kisses along her throat, all over her face. Ashley felt ready to explode.

Leading her toward the head of the bed, he took a handful of foil squares from his pocket and tossed them onto the nightstand. He sat on the edge of the bed and pulled her between his legs. His fingers curled around the hem of her sweater and he eased it up over her head. His hands caressed her breasts through the utilitarian white nursing bra.

"Not the sexiest lingerie," she whispered, then gasped as his palms stroked her nipples.

"You're beautiful, no matter what you wear."

Her heart tightened in her chest at the sweetly spoken compliment. She ached to tell him the truth, despite his likely reaction. She loved him. She wanted him to know.

But then his hand cupped her between her legs and scattered the nascent thought. The clever fingers of his other hand had unhooked the bra, and it fell loose down her arms. His mouth on her turgid nipple completed the connection, driving a shocking orgasm from her.

He turned her, easing her back on the bed. "That wasn't fair," she managed. She clutched a handful of his sweater and yanked it up his chest.

He threw the sweater aside, then stripped her jeans from her. His slacks tossed across the floor, he took a foil square from the nightstand.

As he lay on the bed beside her, she took the condom from him. Tearing it open, she sheathed him, her fingers grazing him, arousing him as he had her. He gulped in air as she took her time with the task, then he pressed her on her back and cradled himself between her legs.

He hesitated, his hand curved around her face. "Ashley…"

Every line of his body screamed his desire, yet still he held back. She stroked his chest, his shoulders, searching his face and finding only more questions. Her hand resting along his throat, his racing heartbeat pulsed against her palm.

"What is it?" she asked, her body throbbing in time with that rapid flutter.

Something hidden behind his dark eyes called to her, a thread of emotion too fragile to sustain itself beyond the moment of desire. It would only survive if spoken out loud, but Ashley knew that would never happen.

His physical release would have to be enough. She pulled him closer, whispering, "Please, Jason."

As he entered her, she knew all the love in her heart showed in her face, as obvious as the sunrise. She couldn't hold back the fire of it. But if he saw it, he chose to interpret it as desire, because he didn't shy away from that overwhelming emotion. He kept his eyes on her, steady and constant. Until she could almost pretend his need was love.

Then he thrust deeper inside her, pushing her over the edge again into paradise. He reached his own climax, holding her so tightly, she thought he might never let her go. Then he pulled her with him as he turned to his side, his arm a pillow for her head, his body still inside her.

He pressed a kiss to her throat, his breathing rough. "Ashley."

I love you. She wanted so much to hear him say it, she said it for him in her mind. For just a moment she would let herself believe.

His lips brushed across her brow, then he rose and went into her bathroom. His leaving triggered a memory of that first time, when she lay there in the awkward aftermath, berating herself for having let herself be intimate with him. But now her only regret was that she couldn't make him feel what she wanted him to. She was happy to give herself to him, if that was the only way he'd let her be close.

The moment he returned, his gaze sought her out. Maybe he thought she might leave him as she'd done before. For the first time, she wondered how he'd felt finding her gone from his bed that night. Guilt twinged when she realized she might have hurt him.

Pulling back the covers, he urged her under them, then climbed into bed beside her. He drew her into his arms, tucking her head onto his shoulder. "That was too fast," he murmured.

"We have time," she told him, although the hours until Sara brought back the twins seemed too short.

He buried his mouth in her hair. "I want you again."

"I'm yours for the next three hours." *I'm yours forever.*

With the first heat of passion satiated, Jason took his time, his kisses long and slow, his tongue exploring her mouth leisurely. His fingers trailed down her arm, lingering at the crook to stroke the tender skin there, then continuing down. He took her hand, bringing it to his mouth to graze each fingertip between his teeth, the tip of his tongue circling her palm.

She could feel him, hard and ready, against her hip. He released her hand, weaving his fingers into her hair to taste her mouth again. His leg between hers, he pressed against her tender flesh, hard muscle and rough hair sensitizing her. Just that contact had her close to the edge.

His mouth sipped along her jaw, down her throat, between her breasts. They ached for his touch, her arousal almost painful as she waited for his mouth, his hands on her. But he held back, kissing everywhere but where she wanted him, his hands brushing with agonizing lightness.

Torn between enduring the sweet torture and taking her pleasure immediately, she grabbed his wrist, holding it, wanting to put his hand on her. His low chuckle told her he knew exactly what he was doing to her, how she was mad with sensation.

She eased her hand lower, along his side, across his hip, his hard-muscled thigh, dipping between his legs. Drawing one light finger along his length, she felt his groan more than heard it and reveled in his response to her. Then his mouth closed over her nipple, his teeth grazing with exquisite care, and she forgot everything but his touch. His leg between hers pressed more urgently against her and her climax caught her by surprise, elevating her to the heavens.

As she shuddered in the aftermath, he reached over her for another condom, protecting himself before settling between her legs again. He eased himself inside her slowly, the strain in his face revealing his fragile control. Once deep inside her body, he stilled, his forehead against hers, his breathing ragged.

"Ashley…" Her name on his lips reached into her heart, as close a profession of devotion to her love-starved ears as he would ever give her. Not enough, but all she could hope for.

Then he moved, his thrusting setting a rhythm that drove her higher again, spiraling up into ecstasy. Her legs around his hips, her arms embracing him, she held on tight to everything Jason would give her—his body, his touch, his heat. For the moment she would forget that she wanted more, that she wanted the impossible.

Her climax hit her so hard, she felt dizzy with the strength of it. Jason's final thrust tipped her over the edge again, leaving her weak and too sated to move. When he rose to clean up, she dozed off, only barely aware of him returning to the bed and taking her into his arms again.

Then she fell into a deeper sleep, a dream flickering in her mind, the images vivid and real. Jason, taking her hands and smiling, joy clear in his face. His voice steady and confident as he spoke. *I love you, Ashley.* She said it back to him. *I love you, Jason.* The words echoed in her mind, in her ears, in the very room as she woke.

Had she said it aloud? Jason had left the bed and stood by the door, dressed again. He stared back at her, his face obscured by shadows. "Did you say something?" he asked.

"No." The truth stuck in her throat. Sitting up, she switched on the bedside light. "What time is it?"

"Nearly six." He started to turn away.

"Jason."

"Your sister will be here soon." His eagerness to leave cut deep.

She pushed aside her pain. "I realize our marriage is…unusual. That you don't—"

"You're right. I don't." All the barriers came up in his face. "I never promised the sex would change anything."

She tipped up her chin, struggling to cling to whatever pride she had left. "If we're going to be intimate, I want you sleeping here with me."

His fingers dug into the door frame, his tension as clear a sign of his reluctance as anything. "If you like."

The stark neutrality of his tone hurt more than anything. "Yes. Please."

He nodded and walked away. Ashley climbed from the tangled covers to shut the door he'd left open.

She'd all but begged him to be a real husband to her, to share her bed, to be at her side when she woke in the morning. Shame stung her cheeks with heat, but she knew she would have asked again if she had to. If she couldn't have his love, she would have his presence in her bed.

She'd eke out what happiness she could from that small crumb.

Sagging against the closed door to his room, Jason tried to wrap his mind around what had just happened with Ashley. Not their lovemaking—although he was still drowning in those sensations—but those softly spoken words she had murmured in her sleep.

I love you, Jason.

She hadn't meant it; she couldn't have. She'd been dreaming, maybe about some other man, had given him his name. That she might fantasize even unconsciously about someone else burned like a private hell inside him, but he found it easier to believe than the alternative.

No one, not his father, certainly not Maureen, not one of the few women with whom he'd had short, unremarkable relationships, had ever said those words to them. He'd accepted early on that there was too much about him that made loving him impossible. The one person who'd maybe loved him despite his uncontrolled energy, his impulsive mistakes, the wrongness of him, his irresponsibility had killed.

That Ashley seemed to like him, or at least tolerate him, had been enough. She didn't, couldn't love him. Because he didn't deserve it. Because he couldn't love her back. He'd given up understanding how that felt, how to share that incomprehensible emotion with someone else.

He heard the doorbell and pushed away from the door. Taking a look at the dresser mirror, he scraped his fingers through his hair to straighten it. He could still feel Ashley's hands on his face, taste her mouth on his. His body responded as keenly as if she was here with him, hard and wanting.

He'd need a dozen cold showers to wash away the scent and feel of her. He didn't have to—she wanted him in her bed, which meant he could make love to her every night. That would satisfy his body, but that tight knot of pain inside would only grow sharper, impossible to release.

If only he could love her. That would make everything all right.

The first week back at school, Ashley cried every morning when she left Marshall and Meredith in the capable hands of Beatrice Farnum, the motherly nanny Jason had hired. Ashley's bright and busy students kept her distracted during the day, keeping her from missing the babies, from tumbling into her despair over her feelings for Jason.

Her students asked a million questions about the twins, endlessly fascinated by the babies she'd carried. They pleaded with her repeatedly to bring them in so they could meet them. She gave in her second week back, arranging with Beatrice to bring in Marshall and Meredith on Friday as a surprise show-and-tell after lunch.

She'd just finished the sandwich she'd brought for lunch in the teachers' lounge when the rattle of the door caught her attention. Beatrice entered, all smiles, Meredith in her arms. Ashley had expected the nanny would bring in both twins in the double stroller. Alarmed, she wondered for a moment if the usually reliable Beatrice had left Marshall in the car. Then Jason arrived, a diaper bag in his hand, their son strapped in the baby carrier.

As every teacher in the room oohed and aahed over the twins, Beatrice made her way over to Ashley. Jason stayed by the door with Marshall, but kept his gaze on her. He'd been gone when she woke that morning, ensconced in his office with the door closed.

Seeing him for the first time today, her heart raced as if she hadn't seen him in weeks, as if they hadn't made love just last night.

Quickly tossing her trash, she reached for Meredith. The matronly Beatrice gave the infant a kiss before relinquishing her. "Mr. Kerrigan suggested he help me bring the twins. He's given me the rest of the day off. I hope that's okay."

"That's fine." Pushing off Meredith's jacket hood, Ashley nuzzled her daughter's fluff of strawberry-blond hair. "We'll see you on Monday."

She walked with Jason across the playground, the iron-gray sky glowering over them. The rain had let up, allowing the students to enjoy their lunch recess outside, but the blustery wind chilled Ashley through the sweater she wore. Jason must have seen her shiver because he wrapped his free arm around her and pulled her close.

Her students were over the moon with excitement, seeing not only the twins but Jason as well, as their surprise guests. Although he'd managed to come into the classroom a few times during the substitute's tenure, he'd been absent since Christmas break. The kids, especially Zak, had obviously missed him.

The little boy clung to Jason like Velcro, the hero worship clear in his eyes. When Jason asked Zak to pick out a book to read, the child dashed around the room indecisively, finally bringing a foot-high stack for Jason to choose from. With one of the little girls cradling Marshall, and Ashley minding Meredith, Jason read a half-dozen books, promising to return soon to read the rest.

"Next week, next week," Zak cried out, jiggling with excitement in his place on the rug.

KAREN SANDLER   217

"That won't work," he said, his gaze meeting Ashley's. "I won't be here."

They finished out the day drawing pictures of the babies, then scrambled out the door as fat drops of rain splattered the playground. With the twins lying on a blanket on the floor, Jason helped Ashley into her raincoat. He brushed a kiss on her cheek as he tugged her hair free of the collar.

"You'll be gone next week?" she asked as she buttoned up her coat.

"Maureen called," he told her, his face twisting with displeasure. "She said a termite inspector found some structural problem in the attic."

"Will that take the entire week?" He hadn't traveled since the twins' birth; she hated to have him gone so long.

With the baby carrier strapped on, he picked up Meredith. "I have to get some issues settled at the home office. I'll be back Friday evening."

Lifting Marshall, Ashley wrapped her son in the blanket. "When are you leaving?"

"Early tomorrow morning. Maureen wants to get moving on the repairs as soon as possible."

As they hurried across the playground toward the parking lot, Ashley felt like her second-graders, upset at Jason's unexpected absence. It would be difficult sleeping alone after sharing her bed with him these past two weeks.

When Steven found out his brother would be leaving for several days, he was as unhappy as Ashley. He made a fuss at the dinner table, refusing to eat the meat loaf and mashed potatoes Harold had prepared, his favorite.

When Jason's reasoning with Steven got him nowhere, Ashley soothed him with a promise that she'd read to him every night, any book he chose. Then it took an hour for Jason to settle his brother, and Harold had to help Ashley get the twins bathed and into their cribs.

Exhausted, Ashley collapsed in bed, struggling to stave off sleep while she waited for Jason to join her. She heard his footsteps climbing the stairs, fought to open her eyes when she heard him enter. He crossed to the bed, standing over her, his face barely visible in the dark room.

"I have to make a phone call. It won't take more than thirty minutes." His fingers brushed her cheek before he walked away again.

Disappointment washed over her. Maybe she would just let herself sleep a bit, then she'd be more awake when he came back. She ought to get out of the sweater dress she wore, but the soft knit was comfortable and warm. She only needed to toe off her flats and tug the comforter over her. She could undress later, when Jason returned.

She seemed to plunge immediately into dreams. The images played out like a movie—a pan up the stairway of the house she'd lived in as a child, the one she and Sara had escaped from. Voices growing louder the higher the camera climbed. Her father's angry roar, her mother's quiet pleading.

Now the camera's viewpoint reversed, to the vantage point of a linen closet at the top of the stairs. That was where she'd hidden, her safe place when her father lost his temper. Usually she had the door pulled closed to keep anyone from seeing her. That night, something— maybe a protruding towel or a set of sheets—blocked the door so it wouldn't shut all the way.

She could see through that narrow sliver to the top of the stairs. At first she only heard the voices—her father yelling, her mother crying. Then the sound of fists against flesh, a body falling against a wall. The scene moved into view when her mother fell to the floor at the top of the stairs. Then her father loomed there, his broad back taut with rage.

Ashley couldn't seem to help herself—she nudged the opening just a little wider. Only five years old, she wasn't brave enough to step out of the closet, to try to help her mother. So she forced herself to watch, to see if maybe there was something, anything she could do.

Shaking, weak, her mother rolled to hands and knees, then slowly climbed to her feet. She swayed, off balance. Her face bleeding and bruised, her blouse torn. Uttering one softly spoken word. "Please…"

The dreams and memories had always fast-forwarded at this point, to her mother at the foot of the stairs, her body too broken to ever be mended. Ashley wasn't sure how she caught that glimpse of her mother's body; she couldn't have seen it from the closet. Maybe she saw her later, before the police came. *I walked away,* Hank Rand had told them. *She must have slipped.*

Except this time the dream didn't jump forward. It seemed to switch into slow motion. Her father seething with incandescent anger. Backhanding her mother with a powerful blow. Her mother falling again, then yanked to her feet by her father.

He threw her down the stairs.

She screamed, couldn't help it, couldn't hold it back. His heavy footsteps clumped toward her, he threw the door open, dragged her out by one small wrist.

At the top of the stairs, he shook her. *You didn't see anything!*

She could see her mother's crumpled body. *No, Daddy.*
He shoved his face close to hers. *One word and I'll
kill you, too.*

Chapter Fifteen

Ashley jolted awake, horror wrenching her from her nightmare. It all came back in a rush now, with certain clarity. It hadn't been an accident. He'd killed her mother.

Huddled in her bed, sick to her stomach, she screamed when the door slammed open. Her father was here! He'd come after her!

Her scrambled brain registered Jason hurrying into the room, his form silhouetted by the hall light. As he sat beside her, she threw her arms around him, burrowing into his safety.

He stroked her hair. "I heard you scream. Are you okay?"

"Y-yes," she stuttered, but her body's tremors wouldn't stop, even with Jason there to hold her.

Pushing aside the comforter, he pulled her into his lap. "Another bad dream?"

She nodded against his chin. "About my mother."

"You want to tell me?"

She took a breath, the truth beating with fists inside her to get out. But a monster's face flashed in her mind's eye, closing off her throat. "When she died…" she forced out.

His hand caressed her back, soothing her. "How did she die, Ashley?"

Tell him! she shouted inside. But her father's evil presence seemed to lurk in the shadowy corners of the room. "Fell down the stairs." The lie tasted bitter in her mouth.

His warmth had started to soak into her, easing her trembling. "Did you see it happen?"

She had to tell him. She couldn't tell him. Her father, maybe dead, maybe alive, still held so much power over her.

The secret tore at her, the horror of it welling up. She couldn't put voice to it, so it erupted in tears, sobs tearing from her throat. Jason held her tight through it all, soaking up her grief and fear.

He grabbed a handful of tissues from the nightstand and dried her face as she cried, even as new tears wet her cheeks again. He no doubt thought her sorrow was only for her mother's death. He couldn't know her terror or the piercing guilt her silence brought her.

When the storm had passed, she opened her eyes to see his all-too-observant gaze on her. "I would never let anything happen to you. You know that, don't you?"

"Yes."

"I will protect you, and the babies." His brow

furrowed, he grazed her cheek with his thumb. "If there was something I needed to know, you would tell me?"

How could she, when telling him might put him in danger, too? Ashley couldn't take a breath out of fear for herself, for him…for the babies. She had to keep the darkness of her past locked away.

She put her mouth on his, hands gripping his shoulders, urging him back on the bed. Straddling him, she grabbed the hem of the sweater dress, jerking it up her body and off. The vee of her legs on the hard ridge of him, she ground her hips as her urgent need to distract him transformed into sensual heat.

Fumbling with her bra, she finally let him unhook it, then gasped as his hands closed over her breasts. Guilt nagged at her, that she was manipulating him, hiding from him. But the only way to stay safe was to keep the truth shut inside her.

When she stripped off her pantyhose and reached for his belt buckle, he stopped her, trapping her fingers. "Slower."

"I want you now," she insisted, fear still driving her.

He brushed a kiss on the back of her hand. "No rush."

Nudging her aside, he rose, pulling off the dress shirt and slacks, skimming out of his shorts. He took a condom from the nightstand drawer and set it aside, then stretched out beside her on the bed. He fitted her into his arms, tucking her head against his shoulder.

"I'm going to miss you," he murmured, his breath fluttering against her hair.

"Don't go." The words escaped without conscious volition.

"It's only a week."

The images from the nightmare rolled through her mind. She clung to him so tightly she was certain she was hurting him.

Easing her on her back, he kissed her with exquisite tenderness, nearly bringing her to tears again. She felt fragile enough to shatter in a million pieces, but his touch was gentle, a whisper on her skin.

Bit by bit, the nightmarish memories dispersed as Jason made love to her slowly, thoroughly. Passion rubbed away the horror, carried her into a welcome oblivion of sensation. He brought her to climax, then before she could fall back completely, took her over that precipice again. Maybe he sensed what hid inside her heart, or maybe he wanted to leave his mark on her before he left. Either way, by the time he pushed inside her, she felt nearly crazed with the heat, too overwhelmed to remain silent.

She couldn't tell him about her father, but another secret pressed up inside, forcing its way out. She climaxed again as he reached his completion, and she could no more keep the declaration inside than she could stop her heart from beating.

"I love you," she whispered. Then, as she tumbled back from the intense peak he brought her to, she said it again, fervently, "I love you, Jason."

At first she thought he didn't hear her. He lay across her, so motionless he hardly seemed to be breathing. His face buried in the crook of her shoulder, every muscle tensed as he slowly pushed away from her.

He lay on his back beside her, still touching her, but a thousand miles away. "No."

Ashley lifted to her elbow, looked down at him. The

light from the hallway barely illuminated his features. "I do. I love you. Denying it won't change that."

He pulled away, heading for the bathroom. "I have to get up early."

When he returned to the bed, he lay beside her, but with his back to her. Undaunted, Ashley spooned up against him, her arm wrapped around him. "You don't have to love me back."

"I can't," he said harshly.

She swallowed back the pain. "Then just let me love you."

He was quiet so long she thought he'd fallen asleep. Then his hand tightened on hers. "I'm afraid, Ashley." The quiet confession hung in the darkness. "Letting you love me..." He brought her hand to his mouth. "She loved me. What I did..."

"You have to forgive yourself, Jason," Ashley murmured in his ear. "You were eight years old. A child."

"It wasn't just her," he rasped out, sounding close to tears. "She was pregnant. What I did killed the baby, too."

His final revelation rocked her. The guilt he must feel, the terrible weight inside him. "It was an accident."

"I have to keep you safe. You and the twins."

"You do," she insisted.

He nestled her hand against his chest. "I'll never let you go," he whispered.

"I won't let you," she said softly.

This will be enough, she told herself as she lay there in the dark, Jason sleeping beside her. Even without his love.

It would have to be.

* * *

He left before Ashley woke, a scrawled note on his pillow. "Call if you need me." She folded the square of paper and tucked it in a drawer.

All day Saturday she waffled between telling her sister about the dream and keeping it to herself. Would it make a difference if Sara knew? Would it impact the way they lived their lives? They were long past picking up and leaving at a moment's notice as they had in the years after their escape. How would knowing the truth behind their mother's death change anything?

When she dug deep beneath her indecision, Ashley faced an uncomfortable reality. A five-year-old's terror still enslaved her. Her logical mind might tell her she could reveal what she'd seen, but irrational fear kept her mute. Her reasons for not speaking to Sara were only justifications for giving in to her fear.

She managed to cajole Steven out of his glum mood by enlisting his help with cutting out flower shapes for a lesson the following week. Then Steven kept an eye on the babies in their playpen while she and Harold made dinner. The call that she hoped Jason would make never came.

It rained on Sunday. Early March proved to be as soggy as the rest of the winter had been. They played Crazy Eights and Old Maid, made hot cocoa and popcorn, and watched a Disney movie on DVD. The phone rang once—Sara calling to chat. They talked about the twins and Evan, about Hart Valley gossip, but the subject of their parents never came up.

Ashley knew she was paying a high toll for keeping the secret to herself. With Jason gone and the hideous images still preying on her, she didn't sleep well from Saturday on. By Wednesday she could barely stay awake in class, despite the noisy boisterousness of a roomful of second-graders held captive by rain. Games of Heads Up Seven-Up could only go so far in containing the energy of the children.

At lunch she lay on the battered sofa in the teachers' lounge and napped. Shadowy monsters populated her brief dreams, creatures she couldn't outrun. When Ronnie, the third-grade teacher in the classroom adjoining hers, woke her, she informed a mortified Ashley that she'd cried out in her sleep.

She dragged herself home, intending to ask Beatrice to stay another hour or two while she caught another nap. But when she pulled into the driveway, she discovered an unfamiliar car parked in front of the house. A man in a chauffeur's suit sat behind the wheel of a black Lincoln Town Car, and he smiled and waved as she walked past.

The only person she knew in town besides Jason with enough money to afford a chauffeured limo was Jameson O'Connell, but pickup trucks were more Jameson's style. Ashley had an inkling of who might be visiting, and she prepared herself for a confrontation as she stepped inside the house.

Beatrice, holding Marshall in her arms, smiled broadly as Ashley entered the living room. "Look who's here—Grandma."

Maureen was holding Meredith, staring down at the baby girl as if she didn't quite know what to make of the pugnacious infant. She lifted her gaze to Ashley, her expression as cold and unwelcoming as it had been in San José.

Beatrice must have sensed the animosity in Maureen. Setting Marshall in the nearby playpen, she reached for Meredith. "I'll take the little angel."

"No need," Maureen said. "We're doing fine."

Beatrice looked over at Ashley. "I can stay."

Ashley crossed the room and plucked Meredith from Maureen's arms. "Go on home. We'll see you in the morning."

Her steps slow and reluctant, Beatrice gathered up her purse and walked out. Ashley laid Meredith beside Marshall in the playpen. "What are you doing here?"

Maureen's nose tipped in the air. "I tried to make things easy for you. I offered you money."

"Which I refused. Don't insult me by offering it again."

"We're past that." Maureen flicked a glance down at the babies. "Do you think he loves them?"

She hesitated only an instant. "Of course."

"You know he doesn't. He's not capable of loving anyone."

The germ of truth in her statement cut deep. "He's devoted to them."

"He feels responsible." She picked her purse up from the sofa and pulled out a wallet. "Maybe I will give you another chance. How much to go away?"

Ashley grit her teeth. "I'm not going anywhere."

"Then we go to option B." She shoved the wallet away and dropped the purse on the sofa again. Her cold blue eyes fixed on Ashley. "Amazing what a private investigator can discover about a person's history."

Unease etched its way up her spine. "I'm not ashamed of anything in my past."

"Your mother dead at such a young age. You had that

much in common with my stepson. Is that what you used to hook him?"

In the playpen, Meredith fussed. Ashley bent to pick up her daughter. "If you think Jason could be so easily manipulated, you don't know him at all."

"I certainly understand your motivation. A pretty little snip like you. You came from nothing, fought for years to survive." Maureen smoothed back her already impeccable blond hair. "And here was your opportunity. A young, rich man comes along who could make your life easy."

Holding Meredith close, she rocked the infant to soothe her fussing. "I told you before, I never wanted Jason's money."

Maureen laughed. "That's what I told Kenneth's mother. She didn't want her son married to a dirt-poor girl any more than I want you married to Jason."

Pity for the woman welled up inside Ashley. "It's too bad the money hasn't made you happy."

A bleak look settled on Maureen's face. "We all make our choices."

Meredith wriggled in Ashley's arms. "Then let Jason and me live with ours."

Maureen's gaze fell on the tiny baby girl, and for a moment her cold blue eyes softened. Ashley wondered if somewhere deep inside this woman a grain of empathy still survived.

Then her mouth hardened, and she looked back up at Ashley. "I know where your father is."

Reflexively, Ashley gripped Meredith tighter. "He's dead."

"I've spoken to him."

A roaring built up in her ears as her knees threatened to give out. She sank onto the arm of the sofa. "I don't believe you."

"Yes, you do." Maureen looked down her nose at Ashley, her expression smug. "Hank Rand is in Southern California, living in a ramshackle motel in east Los Angeles. He was thrilled to discover his daughters are still alive and well."

Suddenly bitterly cold, Ashley shuddered. "Does he know where we are?"

"Not yet."

Ashley surged to her feet. "You don't know him. He's dangerous. Not just to me and my sister but to the twins, as well."

Maureen flinched at Ashley's mention of the twins, then cast that incipient guilt aside. "You're the one who's dangerous. Do you understand how you've put my life in peril? Do you think I have anywhere to go when Jason puts me out in favor of you?"

"He has no intention of putting you out!"

"He's been in negotiations with his lawyer about changing title on the house."

"Why would he do that?"

"Apparently, he wants his happy little family living there. Without me."

Ashley struggled to make sense of what Maureen was saying. "He knows I don't want to live in San José."

"Then he intends to change your mind. That life estate is all I've got. I'll do what I have to to keep it." Maureen's blue gaze grew icy. "Do I call your father?"

Meredith had fallen asleep and Ashley rubbed her chin on the baby's downy hair. "He's an old man now," she said, trying to convince herself more than Maureen. "Maybe it doesn't matter anymore if he knows where we are."

"He's out on bail for spousal abuse," Maureen told her. "This is his third wife. There's some question as to what happened to the second. No one's seen her for four years."

The images swam in her mind—her father's rage, her mother falling. Her blood chilled imagining what her father could do to the twins.

Maureen stepped even closer. "He hasn't forgotten you. Whatever you did to him eighteen years ago, he still remembers. He made that very clear to my investigator."

Her arms shook so badly that she feared she'd drop her daughter, so Ashley carefully placed the baby back in the playpen. "What do you want?"

Maureen's mouth stretched in an ugly smile. "Tell Jason the marriage has been a big mistake. That you don't want him in your life."

"He won't accept that."

"Then you'd better find a way to convince him."

One sure persuasion flashed in her mind, and Ashley's heart contracted in agony. "What about the babies? He won't give them up."

Maureen gave her a long, considering stare. "We'll work out some limited visitation. As long as you're out of the picture."

She felt sick inside. "But I love him."

"Cut the act," Maureen spat out. "That boy isn't worth loving."

Ashley gripped her hands into fists, struggling against the urge to pound Maureen. But that would only make matters far worse.

Tears threatened, but she swallowed them back, determined that Maureen wouldn't see her cry. "I'll tell him when he gets back home."

"No. You call him now." She picked up the phone and held it out to Ashley.

She took it, her hand trembling. "Not with you here. I won't—" This would tear Jason apart; she wasn't about to commit that crime in front of such a heartless witness.

That hard blue gaze narrowed on Ashley. "I'll know if you double-cross me. I'll call your father in a heartbeat."

"Get out of here," Ashley said through clenched teeth. "I'll make the damn call."

Once the door slammed behind Maureen, Ashley almost let her tears fall. But she didn't have the time to indulge in self-pity. She quickly swiped the wet from her cheeks as she pressed the talk button on the phone. As she dialed, she framed the hateful words she would say to Jason.

He didn't answer his cell and she had to leave a message. "Jason, call me," was all she managed before her throat closed up. Then she lowered herself onto the sofa, the phone beside her, to wait for his return call.

The babies had both dozed off in the playpen and she gazed down at them, her love for those two tiny beings overwhelming. How could she take this away from Jason? It would kill him.

But Maureen was right, he couldn't protect them every minute. Her father would always be a threat, looming over all of them—her, the twins, Sara and her nephew, Evan.

When the phone rang, she just about jumped out of

her skin. She could barely stab the answer button, then could hardly speak. "Jason?"

"What's wrong?" he demanded impatiently.

Swallowing, she summoned the words. "I've been doing some thinking. Since you've been gone."

"About what?" There was an edge to his tone.

"When I said I loved you, I shouldn't have. That was just…" Tears stole her voice momentarily. "Just to make you think you really meant something to me."

Silence stretched for several long moments. "It never mattered if you loved me." But she could hear it in his voice. It did matter.

"It was always about the money, Jason. Our friendship. That night in Berkeley." The lie seared her like acid. "When I found out I was pregnant, I figured I'd won the jackpot. But now…"

"No more," he told her harshly. "Wait until I come home. We'll talk then."

She couldn't let him come home, couldn't let Maureen think Ashley hadn't succeeded in driving him off. "I want you out of my life."

"No. I won't listen to this now."

"I thought the money would be enough, but it's not. I want a real life with a real husband." Her heart squeezed so tightly, she thought she'd die. "I want someone who loves me."

"What about the twins?" he asked quietly.

She tried to imagine his face, his response to her apparent deceit. Were his eyes as cold as Maureen's had been, or was the pain clear in his expression? No matter what he might show to the outside world, she was certain of the agony he felt inside, even if he didn't love her.

"We'll arrange visitation. We'll figure something out." Nausea bubbled up. "I have to go. I'll call later."

She disconnected the phone and raced for the downstairs bathroom. The little she'd eaten at lunch came up, leaving her empty and dizzy. It was as if the lies she'd spoken were a poison and her body had done its best to purge itself of its damaging influence.

Stumbling back into the living room, she collapsed on the sofa, shivering and ill. She groped for the afghan throw draped over the back of the sofa, pulling it over her. Still, shudders jarred her body and her teeth chattered.

She needed Jason so desperately, wanted him here, in her arms. In his absence, only one other person would give her strength—her sister. Sara would know what to do next. About their father. About her broken heart. Ashley would call Sara, and once the babies woke up, she would go over there.

Somehow she'd get through this. Somehow the pain would heal and she'd move on with her life. For the babies' sakes, she had to.

But for the moment it seemed her world had ended.

Chapter Sixteen

In that moment his world had ended.

Jason stared down at the cell phone, still in his hand an hour after Ashley had called. If he let it go, set it down, he would lose his only remaining link to her. So he clung to it, a reminder of what he'd lost, of how, in the end, reality had won. He truly was not deserving of the one thing that had more value to him than his own breath—Ashley's love.

Numb, he forced himself to rise from his desk, to fumble for his car keys in his pocket, to walk from his office. His administrative assistant said something to him as he walked past her, but the thunder of stunned grief in his ears washed out the sound of her voice. Time moved in disjointed fashion—he was suddenly in the elevator eight floors down from his sixteenth-floor office suite, then stepping into the basement parking garage, then driving into the last of the late-afternoon sunlight.

He wasn't sure how he made it home—except it wasn't home; home was in Hart Valley, with Ashley— because it was dark by the time he pulled through the wrought-iron gate and up the drive. He had dim memories of meandering through the city, then south on 101 and out to Henry W. Coe State Park. He'd tried to drive one-handed, holding the cell phone, but finally set it on the seat beside him, where Ashley would sit if she was with him.

He was shocked to see it was nine o'clock when he dragged himself from the Mercedes. The babies would already be asleep by now. Ashley was probably up in her room reading or going over her lesson plan for the next day. She'd have her silky red-gold hair pulled back in a ponytail so it wouldn't get in her way.

A knife of longing stabbed him. It took everything in him not to start the car again, head back out and straight for Hart Valley. But what would be the point? Ashley didn't want him. She wanted a real husband. Someone who loved her.

He was at the front door, at the top of the stairs, in his room, time still jolting along, out of sequence. He had the cell in his hand again; he must have picked it up from the seat, although he didn't remember. Maybe Ashley would call back, tell him it was a mistake, that she'd had it right the first time, that she did love him. He was only fooling himself thinking that way, but he didn't put down the phone.

He lay down on his bed, still dressed, the wide

mattress vast and empty. Hours later he fell into fitful sleep, his dreams filled with images of Ashley—running from him, always out of reach, as lost to him as his dead mother.

He jolted awake at just after six, stared dumbfounded at the clock as he wondered where Ashley was. Then he remembered, and his world crashed in on him again.

There was no way he could work today. He had to figure out a way to see her, talk to her. Even if she sent him away, he wasn't sure he could take another breath without the hope of even five minutes with Ashley.

As he stood at the armoire where he'd hung his clothes, trying to force his brain to function well enough to dress himself, it hit him. He'd left things behind in Hart Valley, belongings he had to retrieve. Moving with clumsy haste, he grabbed a dress shirt and slacks, shorts and hurried for the bathroom.

Showered, dressed and shaved, he took the stairs two at a time. He'd made it to the door, had it open when Maureen's shrill voice stopped him. "Where are you going?"

He snagged the raincoat he'd dumped on the floor last night. "None of your damn business."

She gasped, looking as scandalized as he'd ever seen her. "Did she call you again?" she demanded.

"Again?" he asked, hesitating at the door. "What the hell do you mean?"

But she just gave him a scathing look and headed toward the dining room. Jason wasn't about to waste more time on her.

Outside, Jason headed for his Mercedes at a run, but

when he started the engine, he realized the tank was empty from last night's aimless wandering. Leaving the car door open, he dashed toward his stepmother's Lincoln, certain the chauffer would have it gassed up and ready.

He likely broke speed limits twisting through the winding streets toward the freeway, then nearly screamed with impatience when he hit the weekday commute traffic. If the roads were clear, it was a good two and a half hours to Hart Valley. With the clogged interstate, it might take three or four. He thought he'd explode waiting that long to see Ashley.

To redirect the frantic workings of his brain as he drove, he plugged the headset into his phone and called the office. He told his admin he'd be taking the balance of the week off, and the weekend, as well. He'd be in-communicado until Monday.

As he disconnected the phone, Ashley's face swam in his mind's eye. Maybe it didn't matter that she was only with him for his money. Maybe if he tried harder, he could be the kind of husband she wanted. Someone who was devoted to her, cherished her…

Loved her.

It struck him with the force of a hurricane, and it was just as well traffic had slowed to a crawl. He would have had to pull over otherwise.

He loved her. Completely and utterly, without even a trace of second-guessing. She owned every corner of his heart because she lived there, filling up the space inside him with her sweet grace. He couldn't possibly let her send him away because she meant too damn much to him.

She'd just have to accept the fact that he wasn't letting her go. If she truly didn't love him, if his love for her wasn't enough, he'd simply have to find a way to stay near her. He'd live in the guest cottage, he'd buy the house next door. Maybe somehow he'd change her mind.

Once he got past Interstate 580, traffic picked up and he made his way over to Interstate 5 without further obstruction. The trip up I-5 went more quickly, and by nine-thirty he'd passed Sacramento. So focused on Ashley, on seeing her again, the cell phone's ring startled him, sending the Lincoln briefly over the warning bumps.

Snatching up the phone, he glanced at the display. Maureen. He was half tempted to ignore the call. Something told him to answer. "What do you want?"

She was silent so long, he nearly hung up. "There's a problem, Jason."

"Let Renard handle it." His thumb hovered over the end call button.

"I think I might have made a mistake."

In the nearly two decades he'd known her, Maureen had never admitted to being wrong. That she would own up to the possibility set off alarm bells.

His hand tightened on the phone. "What's wrong?"

"Ashley—"

"What have you done?"

"I didn't know," she moaned. "I swear when I went up there yesterday, I didn't know."

"Didn't know what?" he demanded. "Start making sense."

"I hired a private investigator to keep him under surveillance for me. He caught the P.I., beat her…" Unbelievably, he could hear tears in her voice. "She's in the hospital, Jason."

"Who beat her?"

"Ashley's father."

A chill washed over him. "She said he was dead."

"I wish he was."

"Does he know where Ashley is?"

"He made the P.I. tell him everything. Where to find Ashley and her sister. The twins—"

"When?" He wished he could reach through the phone and give her a shake. "How long ago?"

"It was around 2:00 a.m."

"Where?"

"East L.A. He left her in the street—"

Jason disconnected the phone and tossed it aside, checking his watch. Quickly calculating the distance from Los Angeles to Hart Valley, he realized that barring a miracle, Hank Rand was already in Hart Valley. Whether he had already tracked down Ashley was the only unknown.

Groping for the cell again, he kept one eye on the twisting highway as he flipped through his contacts list. He stabbed in the Marbleville County emergency number, his heart pounding in his chest as he waited for an answer.

By the time he'd hung up, he'd been assured Deputy Gabe Walker would head over to the Victorian to check things out. Forty-five minutes later, as he passed Marbleville, the phone rang again. It was Gabe.

"She's not home," Gabe told him.

"At the school?"

"She requested a substitute today. She told Harold last night she had to get away."

"Then she's with Sara," Jason told the deputy.

"We can't find Sara, either."

Fear clawed at Jason. "Did you check the ranch?"

"I'm on my way."

"I'll meet you there." Jason hung up and threw the phone savagely across the car.

Seated beside Sara on the sofa, Ashley clutched her sister's hand, staring at their wild-eyed father as he prowled the kitchen of the quirky octagonal house. The three babies were safe for the moment in the front bedroom, crammed into the playpen together. Hank Rand was still opening and slamming cupboard doors, searching for money or valuables she and Sara had told him he wouldn't find. The gun he'd used to force his way inside was now wedged in his pocket.

Spending the night at the ranch with Sara had seemed like a good idea yesterday. With Keith up in Reno for a few days, Sara was glad to stay over with Ashley and the twins. She understood that Ashley had to get out of the Victorian, away from the myriad reminders of Jason.

Then Hank Rand had arrived. He must have gone to the Victorian first, found no one home. Harold had taken Steven into Sacramento for a visit to the zoo and a movie to distract him from Jason's absence. If they'd been home, if her father had decided to get nasty with them…Ashley felt sick contemplating it.

The years hadn't been good to Hank Rand. In the decade-plus since she'd seen him, he'd lost most of his hair, and alcohol and bad living had marred his face with scars and wrinkles. He was still as wiry as ever, and no doubt as strong as when his favorite sport had been knocking Sara around.

He returned to the living room and stood over them. "Where's the rest of the money?"

Ashley tamped down her anger. "You got everything from both our purses. There isn't any more."

He took a step toward them, and Ashley fought the urge to cringe. "You married a rich guy. There's got to be more money."

Despair filled Ashley at the reminder of Jason. She'd hurt him terribly for no reason. It hadn't kept her or the babies safe. Maureen's evil act had rolled over them with its consequences anyway.

The sound of tires on gravel caught her attention. Hank went to the window. "Who the hell is that?"

Ashley exchanged a quick glance with Sara. "I don't know," Sara whispered. "I'm not expecting anyone."

"Looks like rich boy is here," Hank said. "In a big fat Lincoln."

Ashley's heart slammed in her chest. Joy and fear tangled inside her—joy that he'd come for her, fear for his safety. Did he know her father was here?

As Jason's footsteps neared the house, Hank tugged the gun from his pocket and cracked open the front door. "Don't come no closer, rich boy."

Jason's first impulse was to rush the door, take out Hank Rand before he could hurt Ashley. He didn't give a damn about the gun, would have let the bastard shoot him if it meant he could incapacitate him at the same time. It was crazy thinking, a damn fool idea, but just the thought of the man here filled him with rage.

He took a breath, even as he edged nearer. "What do want, Rand? Money? You want the car? Why don't you just climb in and drive away? The keys are in it."

The gun muzzle dropped slightly as the old creep considered. "How much money you got on you?"

Jason reached slowly for his wallet as he moved to the foot of the front porch steps. "A couple hundred." He slipped the stack of bills from his wallet. "Go ahead, take it."

His greedy eyes on the thick wad of twenties, he let the gun inch lower. "Gimme your credit cards, too."

Jason ascended the first step. His gaze never leaving Hank, Jason thumbed a couple of credit cards from his billfold. "You're welcome to them. But it'll make you easier to track." He sidled up the other two porch steps, now level with Ashley's father.

Hank snatched both twenties and credit cards from Jason's outstretched hand with a quick lunge, the gun pointed down. Letting his rage power him, Jason slammed into Hank, sending him sprawling, and the gun skittered across the porch. He punched the old man, once, twice, before Hank blocked his next blow and threw him off.

He had thirty years on Jason, but he'd learned some dirty tricks in his time. A punch to Jason's gut knocked the air out of him and as he struggled to breathe, Hank's fist pounded the side of his head. Hank's next blow missed when Jason dodged it. He struggled to shove the other man off him.

Right when Hank cocked his arm back to punch again, he froze at the clicking release of a gun safety. Light footsteps moved toward them and there Ashley stood, the gun in her shaking hand, determination in her face.

"Get away from him," she demanded, only the faintest tremor in her voice. "Now."

Hank backed away, and Jason had the distinct satisfaction of twisting the man's hands behind his back. Sara arrived with a pair of leather reins, which Jason used to secure Hank's wrists and ankles. Once he was sure Ashley's father wasn't going anywhere, Jason pried the gun from her hands and reset the safety.

"Where are the babies?" he asked.

"Front bedroom. Meredith will be screaming any minute now."

As they went inside, Jason set the gun aside on the kitchen counter. The twins were still asleep, and Evan lay quiet, fascinated with the mobile clipped to the rim of the playpen.

Assured the babies were safe, he folded her into his arms, pressing her head against his shoulder. "Did he hurt you, sweetheart? Did he do anything?"

"He d-didn't," she stuttered. "Too busy looking for money."

The roar of an engine alerted him to Gabe's arrival. Jason brushed his mouth across Ashley's forehead. "We have to talk." He didn't want to risk saying anything more. They went back outside to meet the deputy sheriff.

Gabe climbed from his car. "Is he here?"

"On the porch," Jason said. "The gun's inside."

As Gabe started toward the house, Ashley stopped him. "I have to tell you about my mother." She took a shuddering breath. "He killed her eighteen years ago. Threw her down a flight of stairs. He made me keep it secret."

Gabe gave her arm a squeeze. "We'll make it right."
He headed toward the trussed-up old man.

The sound of Meredith's indignant squawk carried
toward them. Sara waved them off. "I'll take care of
her." She went inside.

Hands linked, they walked toward the big covered
arena, then out toward the pasture where the horses
grazed. Under the arena's shade he pulled Ashley into
his arms, put his mouth close to her ear.

"I can't let you go," he whispered. "Even if you
don't love me."

She still trembled, no doubt the aftermath of the
horrific encounter with her father. He stroked her back,
reveling in the feel of her. He had to get across to her
there was no way he could walk away from her.

He tipped her head back, drank in the beauty of her
soft brown eyes. "I love you, Ashley. Forever. If that's
not enough—"

"It's everything, Jason." Her eyes burned with an
intense light that reached to his soul. "What I said yesterday…that was Maureen's doing. To keep her from
telling my father where we were. I do love you. With
all my heart."

Elation shot through him, and his throat closed with
emotion. He couldn't remember the last time he'd cried.
Not even the death of his mother had pulled the tears
from him. But now his eyes felt wet, his gratitude for
Ashley's love overwhelming.

Smiling, she wiped away her own tears, the glory of
her devotion to him a miracle. He cradled her face with
his hands. "Tell me again. Please."

She kissed him. "I love you, Jason. Always."

"I love you, sweetheart." He held her close, celebrating her love inside him, their new life starting from that moment on.

Epilogue

"Should I go get it now?" Steven asked, knee-deep in Christmas wrapping paper, the piles of books and video games he'd already opened littering the living room floor.

Ashley glanced over at Jason. Her husband sat on the sofa surrounded by his own gifts, completely absorbed by the autographed science fiction hardcover Ashley had bought for him in San Francisco. She nodded at Steven. "Yes, please."

As Jason's brother hurried out to the guest cottage, Ashley snagged her impetuous daughter before Meredith could take a bite of one of the Christmas tree's lower branches. With both twins walking, they'd decorated only the upper half of the white fir to keep the tantalizing ornaments out of reach. Jason had rigged up a guy wire from the tree top to the ceiling to keep the fir from tipping. Fortunately, it hadn't crossed Meredith's overly active mind to climb the stout trunk.

Marshall had dozed off beside his father on the sofa, exhausted with trying to keep up with his sister. Ashley wished she could curl up and nap next to her son. She sorely missed Harold and looked forward to his return from his visit with his daughter.

Meredith in her arms, Ashley wandered over to the back door to wait for Steven. He crossed the yard toward her carrying the last gift with care, his grip firm on the large, flat rectangle.

"Tradesies," he said, setting the package down before sweeping Meredith into his arms. He carried her back into the living room, seating himself with her beside Meredith's tower of Christmas presents. From the pile of books, he pulled out a fat cardboard tome about puppies and kittens.

With Meredith occupied, Ashley called to Jason from the kitchen doorway. "There's one more."

He looked up from his book and smiled, that curve of his mouth less and less rare these days. "Do we have room for another present?"

She brought the gift to him, placing it into his hands as she fought off a rampant case of nerves. It had seemed like such an excellent idea three months ago when she'd thought of it, a way to give Jason a gift as great in magnitude as the one he'd created for her a year ago. It had become a bridge between her and Jason's stepmother as well, a way to begin to heal the wide rift between Maureen and her stepson.

But now, with Jason looking up at her curiously, his fingers wrapped around the edges of the package, doubt niggled at her. What if the present upset him rather than pleased him? The last thing she wanted was to spoil an otherwise beautiful Christmas day.

He smiled broadened. "Did the twins actually stand still long enough to let you take their picture?"

"Open it," she told him, too anxious to say anything more.

Hooking his fingers into the festive red-and-green paper, he tore wide swaths away. When his hands pushed aside the wrapping to reveal what lay beneath, he froze, staring down at the gift.

His mother, beautiful in her bridal veil, his father handsome in his plain navy suit, the photograph captured Jason's parents in a moment of undiluted happiness. Seeing it again, Ashley reacted the same way she had when she'd first seen the twenty-eight-year-old portrait— with a bittersweet pang of joy. But how would Jason feel?

His smile faded, but the softness in his face told her he wasn't upset at her gesture. He drew a finger across his mother's image. "Where did you get this?"

She sat beside him, squeezing between Jason and their slumbering son. "Maureen, believe it or not. She found it in amongst some of your father's things."

"I remember this photograph. My mother used to keep it on her dresser." His eyes glistened with moisture. "Maureen gave it to you?"

Ashley took his hand. "She wants to make amends. She knows she made a terrible mistake."

Jason's stepmother had made the first move, contacting Ashley several months ago, full of contrition. She understood the danger she'd put Ashley and the twins into and had begged forgiveness.

Ashley brushed a kiss across the back of Jason's hand. "She'd like to see the twins. Have a chance to be a grandmother to them."

He gazed down at his parents' wedding picture. "We can give it a try."

"Thank you." She put her arms around him. "I love you, Jason."

His mouth beside her ear, he whispered the words, "And I love you. Always."

* * * * *

SPECIAL EDITION™

**Bound by fate, a shattered family renews
their ties—and finds a legacy of love.**

Family
BUSINESS

HER
BEST-KEPT
SECRET

by Brenda Harlen

Jenny Anderson had always known
she was adopted. But a fling-turned-serious
with Hanson Media Group attorney
Richard Warren brought her closer than ever
to the truth about her past. In his arms,
would she finally find the love she's
always dreamed of?

Available in May 2006
wherever Silhouette books are sold.

You're never too old to sneak out at night

BJ thinks her younger sister, Iris, needs a love interest. So she does what any mature woman would do and organizes an Over-Fifty Singles Night. When her matchmaking backfires it turns out to be the best thing either of them could have hoped for.

Over 50's Singles Night

by Ellyn Bache

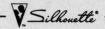

SPECIAL EDITION™

THE **COWBOYS** OF
❖— **COLD CREEK** —❖

Love on the ranch!

NEW FROM

RaeAnne Thayne

DANCING IN THE MOONLIGHT

May 2006

U.S. Army Reserves nurse Magdalena Cruz
returned to her family's Cold Creek ranch from
Afghanistan, broken in body and spirit. Now
it was up to physician Jake Dalton to work his
healing magic on her heart....

Read more about the dashing Dalton men:
Light the Stars, April 2006
Dalton's Undoing, June 2006

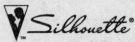
COMING NEXT MONTH

#1753 CUSTODY FOR TWO—Karen Rose Smith
Baby Bonds
It was a double blow to wildlife photographer Dylan Malloy—the sister he'd raised died suddenly *and* didn't leave her newborn in his care. Though her friend Shaye Bartholomew gave the child a good home, Dylan wanted to help. He proposed marriage—but was it just to share custody, or had Shaye too found a place in his heart?

#1754 A WEDDING IN WILLOW VALLEY—Joan Elliott Pickart
Willow Valley Women
It had been ten years since Laurel Windsong left behind Willow Valley and marriage plans with Sheriff Ben Skeeter to become a psychologist. But when her career hit the skids, she came home. Caring for an ailing Navajo Code Talker, she began to work through her personal demons—and rediscovered an angel in the form of Sheriff Ben.

#1755 TWICE HER HUSBAND—Mary J. Forbes
When widow Ginny Franklin returned to Misty River to open a day-care center, she didn't expect to run into her first husband, Luke Tucker—literally. The car crash with her ex landed her in the hospital, but Luke considerately offered to take care of her children. Would renewed currents of love wash away the troubles of their shared past?

#1756 HER BEST-KEPT SECRET—Brenda Harlen
Family Business
Journalist Jenny Anderson had a great job in Tokyo and a loving adopted family, but she'd never overcome trust issues related to her birth mother. For Jenny, it was a big step to get close to Hanson Media attorney Richard Warren. But would their fledgling affair run afoul of his boss Helen Hanson's best-kept secret...one to which Jenny held the key?

#1757 DANCING IN THE MOONLIGHT—RaeAnne Thayne
The Cowboys of Cold Creek
Family physician Jake Dalton's life was thrown into tumult by the return of childhood crush Magdalena Cruz, a U.S. Army Reserves nurse badly injured in Afghanistan. Would Jake's offer to help Maggie on her family ranch in exchange for her interpreter services at his clinic provide him with a perfect pretext to work his healing magic on her spirit?

#1758 WHAT SHOULD HAVE BEEN—Helen R. Myers
Widow Devan Anderson was struggling to raise a daughter and run a business, when her first love, Delta Force's Mead Regan II, suffered a grave injury that erased his memory. Seeing Devan brought everything back to Mead, and soon they were staking a new claim on life together. But if Mead's mother had a say, this would be a short-lived reunion.

SSECNM0406